About the Author

Mike Roberts is originally from England. His father was a proud Yorkshireman, born and raised close to Sherwood Forest. Mike has travelled the world as a non-profit worker and one of his most enjoyable projects involved supporting the YMCA Resource Group on the Environment – a group of young, green heroes from around the globe, determined to change the world. Mike is married to Mary and they both live in Houston, Texas.

Pachamama Protectors and the Planetary Pirates

Michael Roberts

Pachamama Protectors and the Planetary Pirates

Olympia Publishers
London

www.olympiapublishers.com
OLYMPIA PAPERBACK EDITION

Copyright © Michael Roberts 2024

The right of Michael Roberts to be identified as author of
this work has been asserted in accordance with sections 77 and 78 of
the Copyright, Designs and Patents Act 1988.

All Rights Reserved

No reproduction, copy or transmission of this publication
may be made without written permission.
No paragraph of this publication may be reproduced,
copied or transmitted save with the written permission of the publisher,
or in accordance with the provisions
of the Copyright Act 1956 (as amended).

Any person who commits any unauthorised act in relation to
this publication may be liable to criminal
prosecution and civil claims for damage.

A CIP catalogue record for this title is
available from the British Library.

ISBN: 978-1-80439-753-4

This is a work of fiction.
Names, characters, places and incidents originate from the writer's
imagination. Any resemblance to actual persons, living or dead, is
purely coincidental.

First Published in 2024

Olympia Publishers
Tallis House
2 Tallis Street
London
EC4Y 0AB

Printed in Great Britain

Dedication

This book is in memory of Anita and Sid, both great parents and cancer survivors.

Acknowledgements

Many thanks to Mary, the love of my life, for all her support, my good friend Rich and my younger shoulder Mabel.

Introduction

The parents of James and Emma Trueman had a favourite song, 'Big Yellow Taxi' by Joni Mitchell. They played old CDs from their younger days often and there were many classics that the children enjoyed. But their mum and dad's favourite was also their favourite. Originally, it was the catchy tune and Joni's husky voice that had caught their ears – toes tapping and fingers clicking along. Then it was the mental image of a giant, bright yellow taxicab that maybe Emma and James could catch to school one day. Finally, they were old enough to learn the lyrics, singing out loud whenever the song came on and requesting it regularly.

Then one Christmas, after all the presents under the tree had been opened, the brother and sister were told to look out of the front window. There, parked on the street was a real life big yellow taxi! Their father had found a car company in Leeds that owned one and he had rented it for the holiday. The whole family put on shoes and coats, ran outside and jumped in the car. Mum had brought the CD. She immediately put it on and they were off, driving down the street, singing along to Joni.

The whole 'present' was so much fun, but like a lot of things their parents did, James and Emma knew there had to be a point to it. After about ten minutes of driving, they came to a hill and stopped. The music's volume was lowered and Mr Trueman turned around in his seat. "Get ready," he said.

The taxi then climbed up the hill, straining a little because it was an old car, and, at the top, they pulled over again on the verge of the road and everyone got out. The summit of the incline looked out over what had once been a green valley in the Yorkshire Dales. Now, everywhere in front of them was grey. There were roads, housing estates, factories, office towers, shopping malls, smoke, and, of course, lots and lots of parking lots.

Mrs Trueman spoke up. "We just wanted to make sure you really understood the lyrics to the song and that you appreciate how lucky you are to live in Loxley."

Loxley Chase
One

Loxley was not just an average village in England. It was unique. Loxley had kept its leafy history in old churches with lichen and moss-covered gravestones, ivy-covered pubs, and brick houses with lawns, flower beds and thick, thorny hedges. Surrounding towns had knocked their 'relics' down and had been proud to erect new, shiny buildings. Grey and black was their decor, to match the look and texture of the early morning smog. Loxley had managed to keep its air clean. This helped maintain a small, close-knit community feel, with descendants of old Yorkshire bloodlines that had been in the village for centuries mixing with diverse, newcomer families. Both new and old residents wanted a healthy, clean environment to raise their kids. Some things were just more important.

Other villages and towns had suffered from a cycle of upward mobility: individuals and couples leaving for more money, nicer cars, and bigger houses to be replaced by a whole new population on their way up, then another new population – very few people settled for where they were or what they had any more. It was the modern way. Loxley had kept its time-honoured rituals with a cricket team in the summer and football team in the winter, a maypole and dancing in the spring and a big bonfire and burning Guy Fawkes figure in the autumn. Oh, and, of course, Loxley had kept its old forest – more of a wood now – when others had chopped all of their trees down. Loxley Chase sat on a hill at one end of the village, overlooking the community, waving and creaking in the summer winds or throwing brown and crinkled leaves into the streets during winter gales. The shadow of Loxley Chase dominated the village, and maybe this was the reason surrounding populations kept their distance, because Loxley Chase was haunted.

There were many stories that told about the spirits in the wood, fables that stretched back for centuries because Loxley Chase was very old. It had once been extensive, spreading far to the north, and far to the south when it had been known by its previous, more famous name, Sherwood Forest. Those were the days when all of England had been covered in trees and kings and queens ruled over a small and simple population of hunters and farmers. Then that simple population had grown, and axes had turned to chainsaws and scythes had turned to combine harvesters and the forests were destroyed. And as the woods were cut down, so the colours of the world began to drain away.

But Loxley Chase remained, solid and firm and many people said that was why the village was a last fortress of verdant health, because it had ancient trees. The New Forest was gone, Thetford Forest was gone, Kielder Forest was gone but Sherwood Forest remained in the form of little Loxley Chase, which sat stubbornly on a hill despite numerous attempts to cut it down. Every week in the Merry Men pub, old regulars whispered stories from the past in between sips of ale. Some stories were centuries old and told of lords sending their servants to hunt deer or collect firewood only to have them return screaming and crying and begging never to be sent back. Some were decades old telling of factory and mill owners purchasing the land, sending in big cranes and excavators to level the wood, only to find their machines mysteriously breaking down, or their workers falling ill, or employees mimicking those old servants from years past, running and screaming for their homes after staying too late near the trees. Local jokers in Loxley had made lots of money by continuing to sell the old forest to outsiders, knowing that fear and mishap would mean the outsiders would leave and Loxley Chase would remain.

That didn't mean the villagers of Loxley, old and new, were not afraid of the forest. On occasion, daring young men or women, or drunken fools had dared to cross the boundary where green grass turned to thick, dense trees, but all who entered slowly eventually left at great speed and in a panic with new tales of ghosts and ghouls, strange spirits and noises of spirits that meant they would never go close to the Chase again. This happened so often over the years that eventually the ancient wood on the hill was left alone. No one dared to venture even close to the trees, and more and more stories, real and imagined, were told late at night in the pubs and around fireplaces to reinforce the legend. Locals were happy with the magic that coated their village and kept it old, clean and fascinating. If the trees were responsible for that magic, fine. Let them be responsible and undisturbed.

Two

Loxley Chase could be seen from the village school, and, one afternoon, James Trueman was staring that way before a football match against rivals Sheffield High. The wind was swirling, which would make for a hard game, but it also made branches sway and leaves dance, and the sounds that regularly drifted out of the wood even more eerie – groans and creaks and mysterious whispers.

James was the toughest defender on the Loxley team and while he didn't really need any help getting mentally prepared to play against a difficult opponent, it didn't hurt to try and draw on some of the frightening qualities that the old forest possessed. James had become fascinated by the trees in the last few months, fascinated by the lonely vigil they kept on the hill and by the fact that they were unique in this county, this country and even in the world. He had done some reading on ancient forests and they were so rare. Come to think of it, there wasn't really anything green anywhere and that was one reason why his parents loved Loxley, because it was alive.

When you left the village limits, you left unique behind and entered concrete uniformity, condominium complex after condominium complex, office block after office block and road after road. James agreed with his parents and was very happy to be living in their small brick cottage on Old Mill Lane. He liked to be different and

Loxley was certainly different in so many ways.

James carried on looking up at the trees until the whistle blew to start the game and then he focused entirely on the task at hand. He was a good player and his team relied on his strength at the centre of the defence. This strength was put to the test early when the Sheffield team attacked, but a timely tackle here and towering header there meant the initial threats were repelled, and then James was able to sneak forward undetected to meet a crossed ball from his friend Billy and he aimed an unstoppable shot into the bottom corner of the goal to put his team one to nothing ahead.

On another field next to the football pitch, James' sister Emma was playing for the Loxley field hockey team. She was just as athletic as her brother; but instead of being a tough defender, she was a quick and creative midfielder. She provided goal opportunities for others, defended and broke up attacks from the opposition players and raced from one side of the field to the other in pursuit of the ball. It was hard to keep your eyes on Emma as she zipped around, a bundle of energy, perfect for the position she played. During pauses in the game, she often looked over to the neighbouring pitch to see if she could spot her brother in action. James worried her. He had once played his own sport with the fun and carefree abandon that she played hockey, but ever since their father had fallen ill, James' heart had hardened and he seemed to live life with a perpetual frown on his face. His teammates loved the newfound grimness he brought to his game because even more than before, it made him the toughest defender in the league to beat and made opposing players fearful and hesitant when trying to score. This season, the Loxley football team had the best record in the area and it was largely because of the play of 'Chopper Trueman' as her brother was known. Of course, her own field hockey team also had the best record in the area and that was mostly because of the goals Emma either scored or set up for teammates. Loxley had a lot to be thankful for because of the Trueman family. It was a shame that the Trueman family did not feel as thankful about life at that moment. They were going through a very tough time.

Mr Trueman had been sick for more than a year. He had once been a history teacher at the same school that his children attended, and in the same building where his wife had taught English. Loxley Grammar looked like the quintessential English public school, with a red brick great house and smaller classrooms separated by lawns and joined together by winding gravel pathways. Until recently, it was not uncommon for the entire Trueman family to sit on a couple of wooden benches under a tree together at lunchtime, saying hello and eating sandwiches. Mr Trueman was a history freak, always talking about dates and time periods and famous people through the ages. His wife was the same way with literature, reading and quoting prose and poetry at all hours of the day and night. In fact, they had named their son and daughter according to their favourite subjects. Both had been adopted from overseas, specifically from poorer countries. The Truemans felt blessed to live in Loxley but had a global outlook. They had initially been sad that they could not have their own children but then saw it as an opportunity to provide a stable home for orphans who had lost their own families and support systems because of wars or economic woes, mostly brought on by climate change. The world was on the edge of freefall and catastrophes were upending communities everywhere and Mr and Mrs Trueman were determined to help.

Their daughter had been chosen first, from an agency working in India, and the flip of a coin meant that Mrs Trueman got to name Emma after Emma Brown, an unfinished novel by Charlotte Bronte. Two years after Emma's adoption, they had brought home a son born in Poland and, this time, Mr Trueman had chosen the name James after the famous American president, James Madison – also known as the 'Father of the Constitution'. From a very early age, both children were schooled on the achievements of their famous namesakes and were able to quote lyrical lines from Bronte and diplomatic speeches from Madison.

But neither Mr Trueman nor Mrs Trueman had been at school for a long time. When Mr Trueman had been told he had cancer, he tried to work for as long as he could before the illness and various treatments took all his strength away. Then Mrs Trueman had left work to take care of her husband. The villagers tried to pitch in, to support the couple as best they could, but not working meant the family did not eat as well as before, wore hand-me-down clothes and had little time for fun family activities. It was a grim period in their lives. Of course, it was hard on Mr Trueman because he was sick, and Mrs Trueman as she tried her best to care for her husband, and Emma who looked for ways to support both parents and do her share of work around the household. But James seemed to be impacted in hidden ways. He was a fourteen-year-old boy who felt useless. He desperately wanted to help but did not know how to, and, consequently, his mood darkened and relationships suffered. He had lost all but his very best friends because he could not talk to them and they did not seem to understand what was going on in his life. Emma, in fact, had become his closest friend of all. She really did understand what he was going through, and she also managed to maintain a positive outlook which cushioned his own hurt. She was the only one who could occasionally cheer him up, make him laugh, or make him talk, letting his emotions show. James was not like other boys he knew. He was extremely grateful to have a sister.

Three

When James and Emma's father took a turn for the worse and was admitted to hospital, James also took a turn for the worse and his mood darkened even further. It was his black emotions that led him towards Loxley Chase one Saturday afternoon with his sister in tow, arguing, threatening, pleading with him to turn around.

"I don't understand. Why would you want to go anywhere near the wood, James? No one goes there. It's scary!"

"Maybe I want to be scared. Maybe I want to be in a frightening place. And, anyway, how can it be more frightening than the place we're in now?"

James was striding at a fast pace up Loxley Hill, his sister half walking, half jogging beside him. If he wanted to be truthful with himself and with his sister, he didn't really know why he was going to the wood. Lately, he just couldn't stop himself from looking up at the trees. He felt drawn to them and, now, with his father in the hospital, it seemed like Loxley Chase might be the only place where he could rid himself of all the pent-up fury he felt inside. And he had meant what he said to his sister. Could it really be more frightening than real life – a real life where your dad was in hospital dying?

James and Emma reached the outskirts of the wood, breathing hard from the exertion. Their pounding hearts were mostly caused by the steep climb, but they also beat a little faster because of the dark stand of trees before them and the sudden edge they felt in the wind. James paused for a moment, second thoughts threatening to cloud his mind, but then his anger boiled again, and he surged forward, stepping between two oaks into the shadows. Emma called his name before she followed reluctantly behind, trying to keep in her brother's footsteps. While most of the foliage was thick, and undisturbed, James somehow seemed to stumble onto a pathway.

Three startled rabbits shot into the undergrowth and a badger stood on the path for a few seconds, trying to stare him down before darting behind a bush. This nearly brought a smile to the boy's stern face. James loved animals; another reason to live in Loxley. Sightings of wildlife were common, unlike other villages and towns which were lifeless. But three rabbits and a badger, that was unusual.

He followed the path as it continued to weave and wind, the light growing dimmer as the trees grew taller, becoming even more densely packed together. There were rustling, chattering sounds in the wood, chirping from above and scurrying below which again caused James to pause. He had expected to be frightened by spectral sightings of scary dead things, not pleasantly surprised and surrounded by furry and feathered living things. Emma was quiet, content to keep close to her brother while stealing glances at either side of the trail, looking for who knows what but sure that they were being watched by more than birds as they pushed deeper and deeper into a wood that had not seen or heard people for many years.

James' mood had changed from fury to a kind of angry fascination as the trail he was following continued to snake its way around old yew trees, birch trees and, of course, many of the famous English oaks. Mice and voles skittered away from under his feet, and, as he watched them, he was aware that there shouldn't be a trail this worn down in a wood this old and unvisited. But he continued to follow the path nonetheless, eyes alert, heart still thumping. Eventually it curled off to the left and then opened into a large, wide, circular clearing. The floor of the open space was covered in brown leaves along with four solid but termite-riddled logs. Looking up, they could see glimpses of a cloudy sky, but only glimpses, because branches stretched across the gap to form a thick canopy.

Their eyes were soon drawn to one colossal tree that stood in the corner of the clearing and they realised most of the green ceiling came from this tree. It was twisted and gnarled and must have been close to twenty-five feet in circumference, huge branches curling out from the trunk and gradually bending up to the sky, smaller arms shooting off at intervals to follow their own trajectory. Brother and sister stood side by side, staring around and up, amazement and interest overcoming fear. The tree seemed like a natural marvel, but then the whole glade felt like it must be the supernatural heart of the forest. They looked at each other, Emma shrugging her shoulders, admitting without words that she had no idea why this space existed, unless it was just to provide an arena for an oak tree that must have been King of Sherwood way back when the Normans invaded. Realising they were both tired, they sat on one of the logs and whispered.

"How far in did we walk?" James understood now that he had been in a kind of trance as they followed the trail. He also knew that his sister was more attentive than he was, even when he was in a good mood.

"I'm not sure. We must have been going for thirty minutes or so. Quite a way. What is that tree? It looks as though it's looking at us and can hear us. What is this place?"

Both looked around again. The circular clearing was just that, almost exactly circular. It had to have been manmade, but, if it was, other people had been sneaking into the wood unseen for years, and that just wasn't the case. Everyone was petrified of Loxley Chase. It could have been a glade that was hundreds of years old but then it would have been reclaimed by nature long ago.

There were no signs of habitation, no remains of a fire, cooking or bedding and there were no encroaching roots or bushes or vines – just flat, leaf covered forest floor. They both puzzled for a few more minutes, lost in thought until a twig snapped. An instinctive fear washed over them, buttressed by age-old tales. James squeezed his sister's hand briefly for comfort, then they slowly turned around on the log and saw, standing at the back edge of the clearing, a tall shimmering man.

The dread that began to flood both of their bodies – because they were without a doubt staring at a real life, or real dead ghost – stopped almost immediately and changed to interest tinged with excitement. The man before them was not an ogre – far from it. He was a handsome, strong young man with a hint of a smile on his face. He wore olden-style clothing, a tunic of some kind and loose-fitting leggings that were tucked into thick, solid leather boots. Around his neck and down his back hung a cloak and in one hand was a long, sturdy branch, whittled and carved to make what had to be a walking and fighting stick. Beside his feet, more animals stood, sniffed and stared – only the creatures were white, or slightly see through. There were two rabbits, a stoat and a squirrel – spirit animals.

The ghost considered them for a few seconds and then walked forward to stand directly in front of them, scattering the spirit creatures. It was the strangest thing either of them had ever seen. The image before them was grey and white, glistening and flickering slightly at the edges, almost like a cinematic apparition. It certainly wasn't a threatening ghost – more interested and interesting. The silence stretched for another minute, so Emma decided to speak.

"My name is Emma and this is my brother James. We live in the village. Who are you?"

The spectre's smile became a little wider and he said, "I like that you are not afraid. I like that you do not run as the others did, although, in fairness, my countenance was a little different with the others."

James and Emma looked at each other and again. It was Emma that spoke for both. "There doesn't seem to be any reason to run. Do you mean to harm us? Who are you?"

"You are an interesting pair. You are unafraid in different ways. James, you would fight me if you needed to, and I admire that. Emma, you would win me over and make me your friend, but fight if you must and I admire that. I am the ghost of Loxley Chase, of course."

James leaned forward. "Are you Robin Hood?"

The man adjusted his stance and cleared his throat. "I am olde England is what I am, a symbol of what was. I am a green pasture, a stag, a windswept moor, many sturdy oak trees. I am what the world has lost. But can it regain it? I am frightening to most, but not to you. You I like. I would be your friend if you would accept that."

The brother and sister both grinned, excited. "Yes, we would be your friends."

The Ghost of Robin Hood
One

The next day, after school was over, Emma and James went to the hospital to visit their dad. They talked and when he eventually fell asleep, the siblings sat, whispering and pondering on what was a weird time in their lives. It was like they were floating in a neutral zone between two dream-like situations. Here they were, sitting beside a bed in a hospital, with a father who was weak and frail, obviously very sick though he was putting on the bravest face he could for his family. They were close to tears and afraid, but then with a glance, a spark and a shared memory, their moods lifted. Yesterday, only one day earlier, they had been in Loxley Chase with a ghost and now here they were in a hospital room with a father who was deathly ill. James' fury had gone. For whatever reason, anger had been replaced by hope. Yesterday, he just had a dad who was dying and there was nothing he could do about it. Today, he still had a dad who was dying, but he had a friend who was a ghost, a friend who just had to be the ghost of Robin Hood – a legend.

And they had talked with that legend, not for long and not about much, but most importantly for James, about being friends. Who would not have hope the day after they had become friends with Robin Hood?

Emma, as always, was more thoughtful on the subject.

She had been as amazed as James when she woke up that morning and remembered the adventure from the day before. She, too, thought they were trapped in the middle of two mysteries; one, a real life unknown involving their father and cancer; the other, a strange, impossible event involving, of all things, a ghost. What might happen? What possibilities were out there when you knew an actual ghost? Her instincts told her it was a good thing, but it was in her nature to reserve judgement until she had more evidence; and they were going to get more evidence that very evening. This time, though, they were bringing reinforcements. They were not going to surprise the ghost, but, in fact, had asked him the day before if they could return with friends. Knowing Robin Hood, seeing Robin Hood, just seemed like something that had to be shared. He had appeared unsurprised by the request and had said it was okay to bring others. In fact, he thought bringing others would help because he had a task for them all.

But – and Robin Hood had followed his 'but' with a stern look for the first time – if they brought others, they needed to be people that Emma and James absolutely trusted. He was clear that if there was any deception, he would be able to detect it and he would not appear; he would leave them standing alone in the wood. No further explanation was given and they just assumed that ghosts had extra-sensory perceptions. They were ghosts, after all. And James and Emma didn't mind that there were rules. They were just excited, and, that evening, they had an in-depth discussion, trying to make sure the friends they chose were dependable, while also trying to figure out what possible help a ghost might need.

Emma had lots of friends but not all of them were tried-and-trusted friends. Some were superficial and followed her around because of her sports or academic skills, or just because she knew and was liked by lots of people; and it was good to say you were close to Emma Trueman. No, there were individuals she thought she trusted and ones she knew she trusted. Narrowing the list down in the end had been easy. The same was true for James. His mood changes and dark persona had lost him a lot of friends, or so-called friends – individuals who did not seem to care how he felt or what was going on in his life. Like Emma, he also had people who hung out with him because he was 'Chopper Trueman' and was the toughest defender on the football team. Then there were those that had stuck by him and really tried to help him in times of trouble and it was only right that he rewarded them now for that loyalty.

In the end, they had picked two people each. James had chosen fellow football player Billy and a boy called Richard who lived not far from their house and had known James and the whole Trueman family forever. Emma had decided on a teammate also, Leah from hockey, and a girl called Mabel who had only moved to Loxley earlier in the year but was someone she had instantly taken a liking to. These individuals also belonged to the school's environmental club, along with Emma and James and several other classmates, which added to their suitability as choices. The club had been talking about how lucky they were to live next to the remnants of Sherwood Forest for ages, but, like everyone else, had not even considered visiting the wood. Now things had changed.

The brother and sister decided that they wanted to talk to each candidate as soon as possible and that they would each ask the same simple question: 'Can you meet me at Loxley Chase this evening?' It was a first test. They wouldn't say why they wanted to meet and if the person didn't show up, the search would start over. They also agreed that they wouldn't blame anyone who opted out. Who could fault someone who wanted to stay away from a haunted wood? It was a crazy idea to go into Loxley Chase, after all, and to go into the wood to visit a ghost!

That day at school, they cornered the chosen few and asked them the question. It was interesting and a little amazing that each of the people they had selected agreed to come, especially when told it was important and a secret. It showed that the feelings of trust were not one way but shared. At six o'clock that evening, after Emma and James had returned from the hospital, wolfed down some food and raced out of the door, the entire group gathered on the edge of the wood. Each person present looked nervous. Billy was a small compact boy with light brown skin and short, thick black hair. He was the midfield playmaker of the football team who was very skilful and a great tactician. He was a foil for James' toughness, quietly guiding and directing while Chopper Trueman caused mayhem in the opposition ranks. He had confided in James that he lacked confidence in lots of situations, outside of football, and so James had made a great effort to build Billy up and boost his self-esteem. When Mr Trueman got sick, Billy reciprocated, trying to be as supportive as possible.

Leah had never been nervous about anything in her

life, and, in fact, could sometimes be annoyingly self-assured. That was probably because she was so smart. She was a wiz at science and mathematics and always came top of the class when exams were held. Add athletic skills to her intelligence and it was no wonder she was so poised. But that, almost, arrogant composure often masked a more caring side to her nature. In the same way James' friends had supported him through the cancer nightmare, Leah had clearly been more attentive and thoughtful to Emma over the last few months; and Emma loved her for that. As they waited, Leah wore an expression that portrayed wide-eyed indifference, but a twitch on her cheek indicated that perhaps her confidence did not stretch as far as dealing with Loxley Chase or dealing with the demons and fiends that were supposed to be in Loxley Chase. She had long blonde hair that was bunched in a ponytail – a ponytail that was being distractedly pulled and tugged as she, too, stood some distance from the trees.

Richard was tall and a little gawky. This was definitely an adventure for him because he spent most evenings and weekends at home taking care of his parents who were old and quite sick. They had tried for children for most of their marriage and eventually used 'in vitro fertilization' to have Richard when they were in their late 40s. They suffered from various allergies and ailments and found it hard to be outside so Richard stayed in and helped. He didn't mind being a caregiver because he was into medicine, which was a passion that also helped James as he tried to understand his dad's cancer diagnosis.

Finally, there was Mabel, who was probably the least nervous of the four newcomers standing next to the trees.

She had not grown up with the Loxley Chase legend and the shadow of the wood looming over everything she did as a child. She was tall and slim, as tall as James and Richard, with a skin tone that was a slightly deeper brown than Emma's. Her father was a well-known rugby player who had played for the London Harlequins team but had just been transferred to Sheffield Eagles. Emma and Mabel had first met when the new girl volunteered in the first-year homework room and Emma had seen how patient she was with younger children. Then, when both were walking home one night, a couple of boys had tried to pick on them and before Emma could move, Mabel had kicked one and punched another, sending them running. She was kind but also super tough, which was a great combination!

Perhaps, getting some friends together to stand outside of the wood had been the easy bit. Now, James and Emma had to persuade the group to walk into the trees. They had thought long and hard about this, trying to come up with a convincing story or plan, but, in the end, had decided that the truth was probably the best story they could tell. So, Emma rubbed her hands together once, took a deep breath and tried to talk using her most confident tone.

"Well, I'm sure you're all wondering why we are here tonight." Now she sounded more like a television presenter than a friend, so she coughed and took another deep breath and started again. "You all know that our dad is sick. The other day he was taken into hospital and for reasons I'm not even sure of yet, James decided he was going to walk into Loxley Chase, because, of course, that would make anyone feel better." General laughter resounded and elicited a sheepish grin from James. Now the talk was going better. "Well, we saw something, met someone in there and we decided we wanted to bring some friends with us next time to share the experience—um—decide how to best understand the experience. Oh, what the heck, we wanted strength in numbers to make sure we were brave enough to go back in there." Not exactly true, but Emma was trying to think of inspiring things to say.

The laughter was more strained this time as their friends tried to work out who or what the 'someone' was that they had met. As the moment to actually enter the wood drew nearer, group jitters seemed to be getting worse. Seeing the hesitation, James stepped forward to stand next to his sister. "Look, I like Loxley and it's the best place to live in the world, but I spent a lot of time wishing something different would happen. Then, my dad got sick and I spent every minute wishing ordinary would come back. I know you all feel the same, about things being different that is, not about Dad's being sick." James slapped his thigh in frustration, trying to make the words coming out of his mouth make sense. "Anyway, Emma and I agree that the only thing that has made these last few months bearable is you lot, our friends. So, we wanted to thank you and to share something not ordinary with you, to take you in the wood and let you meet the ghost of Robin Hood! Who wouldn't want to meet Robin Hood?"

There were looks of surprise, mixed with disbelief, that changed to interest when the group realised that this was James speaking to them. James was not a joker or a liar. There was no one more serious in Loxley than James. Emma tried to seal the deal while they had their attention. "I'm not as sure as James that it's Robin Hood in there, but

I do agree with him that you're our best friends and we need help. Will you follow us?"

There were glances all around, more hesitancy as everyone looked for someone else to speak first. Then, they looked at the trees and tried to imagine walking into the trees to look for a ghost. Confidence was draining again and Emma thought they had failed until Mabel cleared her throat and spoke. "I must admit I'm scared, but I'm also kind of pleased that when you needed help you chose me, so I'll come." She stepped forward to stand next to Emma and James and the fact that there were now three people looking at three people seemed to tip the balance. First, Billy half raised his hand and joined the team and then Leah shrugged and did the same, and then Richard took a long stride ahead to make it unanimous.

Emma and James gave each other the briefest fist bump and then before anyone could change their minds, they stepped into the trees. Immediately, they heard an owl hoot from a branch above and a pair of foxes barked and stared out of the undergrowth with distinctive, oval red eyes. The newcomers froze as one for a moment, then slowly continued forward.

The pathway was there just like the night before. James and Emma, feeling their own excitement growing, ushered their friends forward. The going was a little slower, in part because James was not as angry as he had been the previous day, but also because they had four more, somewhat reluctant and certainly apprehensive, people that needed to be guided. The air was full of the same eerie chattering and rustling that the brother and sister remembered, but there was comfort in a crowd; and as the newcomers became more used to the thought of being in Loxley Chase, the speed increased. Left and right and back left again the trail wound as they marched forward in single file, startling birds out of branches and rodents into bushes. Then, eventually and quite suddenly, they emerged into the clearing.

The four new friends gasped in unison. Emma and James looked around and realised again just how impressive this natural space was. It was a wooded arena – sheltered but open, big but somehow cozy. And there in the corner was the great oak. Everyone present wandered around the edges and stopped in front of the giant. They stared, fascinated, looked up at the curved 'ceiling' of branches and then, like the brother and sister the night before, sat on the fallen logs to soak in the experience. Silence settled on the enclosure, with even the birds hushed for a moment. And then a throat was cleared behind them and all heads turned in the direction of the noise.

The appearance of the spectre could not have been more effective and impressive. Four sets of eyes were wide open and four jaws had dropped low as the friends gawped in awe. The ghost looked taller, more handsome even than the day before. He shimmered and glowed and it seemed like he was putting on a show as he walked forward and threw open his cloak, revealing a sword and scabbard at his waist that had not been there before. Walking with him was a white fox and on his left a beautiful, glowing female deer.

As the four newcomers continued to stare with fascinated wonder, the spectre turned his head slightly towards Emma and James and winked. Yes, he was putting on a show, in honour of their return and in honour of the companions they had brought with them. The brother and sister would agree later that this was the moment – the wink and the performance – when they truly felt friendship towards a ghost. It was also the moment when they first wondered why they had been chosen, why this man from the past had revealed himself to them.

Two

The friends had rearranged the logs so that they were in a circle in the centre of the clearing, and they were all now seated, including the ghost. His calm expression, and the peacefulness that radiated out from his body along with that otherworldly glow, had reassured the group and put them at ease. Emma and James were proud of the gathering they had put together but were also filled with a sense of anticipation. They, more than anyone present, wanted to hear what this mysterious ghost had to say, but before he could open his mouth to begin, Leah jumped in first.

"Are you really Robin Hood?" Everyone looked at the girl, not necessarily surprised that her supreme confidence had returned – maybe more impressed that it had returned in a haunted wood. Then all eyes turned back to the ghost with interest. They all wanted to know the answer to that question.

The ghost smiled and shook his head. "It's been so long. I had forgotten how curious and direct young people could be. I gave an answer last night to James and Emma but it was cryptic. You need to know that my role here is to be the spirit of Sherwood, protector of the beasts and birds that shelter under the sacred trees and of the trees themselves. But, yes, when I was whole and walked the earth, I was Robin Hood."

A collective sigh echoed around the chamber of trees. What a bonus. What a coup! This was so worth walking through a spooky wood for. And then a frown appeared on their friendly ghost's face and an instant chill blew into the enclosure making everyone shiver.

"Be aware that you are the first people in many centuries to meet me. Be aware that you are the first people ever to meet me after my death and in this form. I have put my trust in you. Others I have scared away, and I could become that frightening ghoul again if I so choose. Is my trust misplaced?"

Emma and James hoped with a passion that they had chosen their friends well. Fear had appeared again briefly on faces and even Leah looked unsure. But as sharp minds processed the information, proud and honoured looks appeared. The initial thoughts of all, maybe understandably as they sat before the one and only Robin Hood, had been about the story they could share with others – the prestige that would accompany the telling of this tale. But the ghost's warning, frightening as it was, had also revealed how lucky they were to be sitting where they were, listening to who they were listening to. They had been chosen and were now friends with the greatest British folk hero ever. Yes, they could be trusted! Who would want to spoil this!

The ghost seemed happy with the reaction he could see on the faces before him, the reaction he could sense in the air. "There was a reason I picked Emma and James for this task. They have sound judgement and they have good friends. Tell me, each of you, what is your ancestry? I am intrigued. I have been a ghost for too long. When I considered this plan, I think I was expecting to recruit a team of Anglo-Saxons. Your heritage seems richer and more diverse, which is good. You will soon meet some of my friends and they are a worldly bunch."

Emma was about to go first but paused for a second as she absorbed Robin Hood's statement about meeting his friends. Then, she focused, stood and spoke. "I was born in India. I didn't ever meet my real parents, but Mum and Dad said the orphanage told them I came from Mumbai."

James got to his feet next. "I didn't meet my parents either, but they were from Poland."

"I am a Chinese American, born in New York. My dad is in finance and we've been in Yorkshire for five years." Billy pointed at a New York Yankees baseball hat on his head and grinned.

Mabel then stood and took a deep breath. "My ancestors were from Kenya and were taken to the West Indies as part of the slave trade. My grandparents came to England during World War II and I was born in London."

Leah got to her feet next and reached out a hand, pulling Richard up too. She then linked her arm in his, making him blush. "I guess we are the least well-travelled members of this group, Richie. We are both born-and-bred Yorkshire folk; and I know for a fact Richard was born just one street away from me in Loxley." The pair high-fived each other before sitting back on the logs.

Robin Hood gave a quick round of applause as the group finished describing their backgrounds. "You are a unique team in many ways. I am more excited than ever to spend time with you and to try and get your help. But I'm sure you have questions for me. Ask away."

Heads again turned as the gathered group looked for inspiration and courage to be the first to ask a question. Mabel eventually spoke up. "I've read a lot of different opinions about whether you were real or not. Many people say you were just a legend."

It wasn't really a question, but the ghost nodded as though it was a good point to bring up. "Most stories from the past have some basis in fact. The fact may be small, but there is something that inspires the story. In my case, most of the story is true although it has been romanticised. There was a lot more mud in Sherwood Forest than the tales reveal, and it was cold at night." Robin Hood grinned, attempting some levity to further ease the tension. "The reason the story began to be questioned was because it was a story of strength, a story that could do damage to those in power. So, those in power questioned it and began to spread rumours that it was false. No, most everything was true."

Richard forgot himself and raised his hand as if he was at school, before his face turned red and he dropped his arm to his side quickly. "What is it like being dead?"

The spectre frowned and leaned forward, putting his elbows on his knees, scratching his chin thoughtfully. "Well, that is a harder question. I mentioned you will soon meet some of my friends and I think they can help me answer that more completely. But, for now, I'll provide some basic thoughts. Everyone who was ever born, and everyone who has ever died, still exists. The Otherworld has a different function than planet Earth. It is a place to 'be' rather than to 'do'. Remember, there is no need for food, drink, shelter or travel, so no commodities to produce. Inhabitants have a chance to exist in tranquillity, without having to strive or achieve. They can reflect on their former lives, enjoy achievements, or perhaps forgive themselves for past transgressions. For many, death is a soothing existence; for others, it involves regret and remorse, anger and pity. Some are accepting, even welcoming of their new after-life and some reject and are jealous of their former lives and those who still live them. Certainly, there is no reason to be afraid of death. It is merely another level of existence."

The friends took time to try and grasp this description – to understand what this Otherworld felt like before Emma decided to move on with another question. "Why are you here on Earth, Robin Hood? And why did you decide to appear in friendly form to us?"

The spectre stood, reached down to his waist and, in one swift movement, drew his sword with a musical ring that hummed around the clearing. Everyone stared in admiration at the shining, bright blade. It gave the scene before them even more of a mystical air. "I need help," he said, looking pointedly at Emma and James, "and I think you need help too."

He walked forward and held out the sword, pointing it first at Emma. "In my time, oaths were important. I think they are not so any more but still we will take an oath. Let us meet when we can, and, if you are willing, I will prepare you. When I have complete trust in you and you, in turn, have complete trust in me, then I will tell you how you can help me. The world is in peril and there is a need to expand the role I have in Sherwood Forest. That is all I will say for now. But" – the ghost looked around at all the assembled faces – "our meeting and this place remains a secret. Outside of this group, this band of men and women, no one will know what we do and what we plan. If you agree, reach out and touch this blade and say 'on Excalibur I pledge'. You will be declaring allegiance to this group."

Beginning with Emma, Robin Hood pointed the sword at each of the friends in turn, and each in turn reached out a hand to touch the tip of the weapon and to say the pledge. There were looks of wonder as the name 'Excalibur' registered and when the ghost saw this, he smiled broadly. "This is good. My trust is growing already. Leave now and return once a week every week until we are ready."

Leah could not resist saying one more thing. "Maybe we can have a name for our group. I know you had your 'Merry Men' when you were alive, but none of us are men and some of us are girls. At school, we have a club that is focused on ways to save the planet and we have been thinking of a few different names. You have been trying to save Sherwood Forest and it feels like there may be bigger green goals to come. Can we use one of the names for our group? My favourite is 'Pachamama Protectors'. What do you think?"

There were lots of nodding heads, but all eyes turned to Robin Hood. Emma offered an explanation. "Pachamama is a name used for Mother Earth by the Inca people in South America. We learned about them in class one day."

The ghost re-sheathed his sword. "This is perfect. Sherwood Forest is the starting point, but the threat is worldwide. Having such a meaningful name will help us remember how meaningful our work is." The newly-named band of friends cheered loudly, and Emma and James gave each other a quick hug, full of hope and anticipation.

The Pachamama Protectors
One

The newly established Pachamama Protectors decided they would meet at the weekend to avoid clashing with school activities or homework nights. A rhythm was soon established and every Sunday afternoon, Robin Hood's band would gather at the bottom of Loxley Hill. They were careful with the tale they told their parents, that they were walking to the high street to meet and hang out with friends. They were pleased when they heard of phone calls being made by parents to parents, pleased because each concerned mother or father heard the same story and so were convinced and relaxed from then on. They were careful not to be followed to the hill or up the hill though not as worried once they had made it to the wood because no one who lived in Loxley or knew of Loxley Chase would dare go near the trees let alone walk into the wood itself.

Every week, they would meet with a ghost – a legendary ghost of a legendary man, Robin Hood; and as if that wasn't a dream come true on its own, once they had all gathered in the clearing, they would plunge deep into history. Their leader explained that he was going to teach them how to survive like outlaws, not because they were going to live in the forest, but because he felt they needed to be ready for a chapter in their lives that would be unlike anything they had experienced before. They were going to understand how to hunt and fight like his 'Merry Men' of old, build character and cohesiveness as a team and perhaps, above all else, learn about the power of Sherwood Forest. To this end, Robin Hood made it clear that it was important that they worked on these skills in Loxley Chase, because the forest itself could teach them.

"The great tree in the corner is called the 'Major Oak' and is over a thousand years old. It is a symbol of the power of Mother Earth and a sign that despite the effects of modernization and climate change, her magic still exists. I am eventually going to teach you more about that magic and how it can help you. The path you have followed and this enclosure are also signs of our ancestors' foresight and their link to the natural world. I told you that the climate disaster was foreseen; so was the understanding that young people would be key to the survival of the human race and that they would need to gather and plan. These same trails and meeting places are in all of the surviving forests, watched over by their own local and mighty trees."

The friends did not really think too much about the reasons for training – they were just amazed at their luck! Each time they came to the wood, there would be an array of weapons waiting for them to admire and then use. There were swords, dull and chipped but also ancient and remarkable – each one dripping with history; staffs, made of different types of wood – each worn down by the sweat of ancient hands; and, of course, a variety of bows and arrows. They would pair up and parry and thrust, swing and block, boy and girl alike revelling in the feeling of strength and glory that came with using an olden day weapon from the Middle Ages. They learned how to hold a sword, shoot a bow and wield a staff, then listened to descriptions of fighting techniques and battle strategies. Robin Hood would wander along the row of new recruits and advise and praise and critique occasionally but with a caring tone to his voice that encouraged everyone to do better if they could. Mixed in with combat training, they learned to make use of natural resources, making shelters, tools and cooking on an open fire.

As these practice sessions developed, the individuals, who had been friends with Emma and James and not necessarily friends with each other, became more of a group, learning about each other as they learned about survival skills. Between activities, the boys and girls would talk and share backgrounds and stories and, eventually, as the training progressed, personalities and habits became more obvious. Everyone knew that Richard was more of a healer than a fighter, so his hesitancy with weapons was not necessarily a surprise. What was a surprise was how good he could be when he found a patient teacher. Often, that was Robin Hood himself, or many times that would be Mabel. She had demonstrated a level of patience with children to Emma when they had first met but also ferocity in a fight. Now, she showed both attributes, calmly teaching Richard the techniques needed to use a long, smooth staff made of ash before inspiring him and demonstrating how the weapon could really win a fight, brandishing it with scary power and speed in a sparring match.

Leah, as well as being an athlete, was interested in the

science found in a battle and would often stop the pretend sword fights to talk about angles and the force of each hit and the amount of energy used by each muscle when wielding a sword. One time, she was so engrossed in a discussion about some theory or other, eyes closed as she tried to remember a particular biomechanical adjustment, that she didn't notice everyone else leave to hide behind trees, giggling quietly, peeking from their hiding places. Leah finally opened her eyes and looked around bemused until the rest of the band burst out into the open, laughing and making fun of her seriousness.

Billy's organised, tactical skills on the football field showed up in an interesting way in Loxley Wood. He brought his own bag of tools with him one day and used a chisel and some sandpaper to smooth out the logs, making them more comfortable to sit on, then sewed together two old tarps to wrap around the weapons so they would stay dry at night. He was something of a neat freak, a trait he blamed on his father and his fastidiousness in their workshop at home. This manifested itself in the forest with him constantly dusting and wiping down the old swords they were using and regularly sweeping the floor of the clearing. Robin Hood thought this was going a little too far and launched into a description of how grim and grimy life had been for himself and his 'Merry Men' back in the days when they were hiding out in Sherwood Forest from the Sheriff of Nottingham and his soldiers. Of course, whenever the greatest outlaw ever reminisced, it was fascinating to hear and the group often tried to steer Robin away from practicing and more towards storytelling. Listening to the classic tales and legends that were known by people around the world, told by the man himself, was just too good an opportunity to miss.

Emma and James, the brother and sister who had made all of this happen, remained the unspoken young leaders of the protectors; and as their confidence grew, their own personalities became pronounced. Emma had no time for the usual stereotypes of girls. She was the bravest and toughest warrior at every practice session and showed all her athleticism in every skill that was demonstrated to them, working until she was sweat-soaked with aching muscles. It became clear eventually that she was a natural captain, helping like everyone else, but demonstrating and encouraging with a passion and skill that was unlike anyone else.

Obviously, she had some extra quality in her character because people responded to her like no other. James was his sister's equal as a fighter – but through ferocity, not necessarily talent. He still channelled all his pent-up anger into practices, unsuccessfully trying to push aside the plight of his father. Often, the others would sit and watch as he sparred with Robin Hood, demonstrating a fury and strength in his moves and actions that was impressive and intense.

The group trained and developed as a team over time and became more and more relaxed in Loxley Chase with a ghost as their teacher. Robin Hood continued to emphasize the presence of a natural force in the wood, the presence of Mother Nature, and this concept revealed itself with more clarity when he showed them how to use a bow and arrow. Of course, archery was what personified Robin Hood; and as he focused, ready to shoot, his very being seemed to glow brighter than ever. He held aloft a shimmering bow, put in place a glistening arrow and from the back of the clearing aimed through the narrow gap that led to their trail. There was a thick oak tree about two hundred yards in the distance where the path made its first turn and the ghost aimed calmly and quickly and unleashed an arrow that threw off sparks in the failing light, shooting through the air with remarkable speed and buried itself in the dead centre of the tree.

It looked easy but when they each took turns, the friends found that pulling back the string alone was a task. Each of the bows they used to practice with were made from long, supple and strong yew tree branches. The strings were like a linen or hemp material, fibre wound tight and then covered in wax, and the arrows – yew also – had a sharpened flintstone on one end and trimmed feathers on the other. As was now usual with this group, Emma stepped forward to try her bow first, standing on one side of the clearing and aiming for a tree directly across. If it wasn't for the fact that each of the band members were equally nervous, she might have been embarrassed by her first attempts. First, an arrow fell straight to the floor, then the string twanged with the arrow still pinched between her fingers; but Robin Hood was patient and eventually an arrow flew from Emma's bow and landed short in the dirt but close to the tree. All of the friends had similar experiences with Leah being the most successful. She seemed to grasp the technique of holding the weapon and the trajectory needed to make the arrow go where she wanted it to go. Third try and she hit a tree just next to the one she had been aiming for, the arrow holding fast in the wood.

Then Robin Hood asked the group to close their eyes, sit cross-legged on the floor and put their hands down to feel the leaves, twigs and soil. "There has always been power in nature and in the earth itself – obvious power, in the beauty we see and the life that exists all around us, but also a deeper energy. Certain individuals and groups have been aware of and have used this energy for centuries. Shamans, healers, ancient hunters and gatherers. Because of the crisis we face, because of the location you are in, and because of who you are – Pachamama Protectors on a quest to save the Earth – that magic is more available than ever for you to grasp and use. Listen." A wind picked up high above them, rocking the trees and causing leaves to rustle and branches to creak. These sounds were joined by chirping crickets, the howling of a wolf, a plaintive screech from an eagle or hawk way up in the sky looking down on the wood, and the snuffling and grunting of a wild boar. Each of the team members heard the sounds and felt an energy creeping up their fingers, then their wrists, then their arms. It was a warm feeling, not harsh or abrupt, but almost like they were being charged, energised in some way.

"Now, stand up each of you and be archers." Emma got to her feet first and picked up her bow. "Remember, you are irretrievably linked to this forest. The bow is made from its branches. It was made by a faithful son of Sherwood. The objective of your aim is the sister of other trees in this wood and it welcomes your arrows. The air and sunlight your missile flies through are like food and drink to the plants. Relax and allow yourself to be helped by the world that surrounds you." Emma took Robin Hood's advice and relaxed in position. As she pulled the string back, she took a deep breath and fired. Bright white sparks immediately flew from her arrow and it shot straight with a slight arc and thudded into the heart of the target, causing her to whoop with delight. James went next with the same result, then Mabel, Billy, Leah and Richard. It was truly remarkable.

The friends laughed and high fived each other then turned to Robin Hood who had a broad smile on his face. "Very good. Now, remember that feeling. Remember how your heart, body and mind harnessed the power inside you to achieve that feeling. And let's see how you manage using other weapons."

The protectors grabbed swords and staffs and paired up, thrusting and parrying with excitement and passion – and with an obviously increased level of skill. Some of the techniques Robin Hood had demonstrated now came with ease and the energy needed to sustain high levels of defence and attack were ever-present to draw on. They each felt like they had gained a sixth sense, providing them with added strength and knowledge as they were sparring, but also an awareness outside of their activities – to smell and hear and sense the living, breathing, growing surroundings that enfolded them.

This was how they spent their time together, every Sunday night, learning and growing and enjoying themselves so much that the days and weeks seemed to fly by. Their skill levels increased along with the respect they held for each of their comrades – and the growing love they felt for their mentor. There wasn't an hour that passed by when one of the friends didn't pause to reflect on where he or she was, to marvel at what he or she was doing and to take a deep breath and stare at this guide who was a ghost. If only these training sessions could last forever.

Two

Inevitably, though, there came a time when the group's curiosity overcame their sense of contentment. It was Emma who finally asked the question that had been in the back of everyone's mind.

"You mentioned help. When we first got together, you said that you had chosen us because you needed help. What is the task you have for us?"

Robin Hood scratched his chin. He had a light beard on his face and as he scratched, Richard couldn't help wondering how ghosts shaved. "I'm glad you asked this question. It's time we moved to the next stage of our training and it's time you understood why we have been working so hard. There is some help I am going to need to make sure you get a clear explanation. Give me a moment."

The ghost was sitting on a log, opposite the protectors and they watched as he closed his eyes, bowed his head and muttered something under his breath. When he looked up again, he winked and then, a few seconds later, there was a rustling in the trees and a second spirit appeared – a young woman, perhaps in her thirties. The friends all stood, more in shock that there was another ghost in their midst than out of respect. The woman smiled, gestured to them to sit, and joined them on the logs.

"Everyone, this is Ada Lovelace. She was one of the

most respected mathematicians in her day so she is far more qualified than me to explain one important aspect of our mission."

"It is very nice to meet all of you. Robin has spoken a lot about his 'Pachamama Protectors'. I must say I do like the name! Well, I know you are all anxious to keep learning, so I'll jump straight in." Ada Lovelace stood, cleared her voice and began to pace with her hands clasped behind her back. She looked like a lecturer in a classroom and clearly found passing on knowledge a serious business.

"There is a concept that you may have read about or if not, Emma and James, perhaps you could ask your mother and father about it. Robin has told me they are teachers. It is called the 'Multiverse Theory'. It means instead of what we used to believe, that everything in existence is contained within our one universe, there are multiple parallel universes and parallel dimensions. It is considered just a concept because, while many scientists are confident the existence of other universes has been proven using mathematics, the idea cannot be proven in any conventional way. We cannot see these universes, hear them, or touch them, which means non-scientists are sceptics. There has been similar confusion in the past before modern scientific equipment and techniques for study existed. We once thought, for example, that our Earth was at the centre of everything and then found out we were wrong. It was just one planet in a vast Solar System. Now the idea that our universe *is* everything that exists is also thought to be wrong."

Billy raised his hand. "They talk about the multiverse

in Marvel comics and movies. Is it the same thing?"

Ada Lovelace nodded and replied with seriousness, "I don't know much about comics or movies. I do know that the intricacies of the multiverse are not easy for everyone to understand so perhaps drawing cartoons and telling stories about it helps. For scientists, we explain things best using mathematical equations and physics formulas, which is why it is one of my specialties. I am also knowledgeable on this topic because there is one parallel universe which is called the Dimension of the Dead; and, of course, I am dead!"

There were frozen expressions on each of the friends' faces as they tried to absorb this last statement. "Wait, say that again?" Even Leah was confused.

"That's okay. This is a tricky subject. Robin Hood and I will give you a practical demonstration." Ada Lovelace nodded to the archer who began walking over to the Major Oak and back again. "Leah, how many dimensions are there?"

Leah was excited to be answering questions for such a famous scientist. "There were thought to be three dimensions – height, width and depth – but then Einstein came up with a theory that time should be included, too, as the fourth dimension."

"Excellent, Leah. I may recruit you as my assistant." The young girl blushed bright red. "Einstein made the point that with three dimensions, we can calculate anyone's position on Earth, except for one thing. Look at Robin Hood as he walks. He is at the oak tree now, but thirty seconds before he was also at the oak tree and thirty seconds later he will be there again. To be completely accurate giving someone's location, we must provide specific physical measurements but also the specific time when the measurement occurred."

Robin Hood began walking again and Leah said, "That makes sense. So, in geography, we use longitude and latitude. And if we were measuring here, we would give the longitude and latitude of the Major Oak, but also when Robin Hood was standing there. So three thirty-five p.m."

"Perfect again, Leah. Now, keep your eyes open and minds focused, and I think you will be the first living people to truly understand the Dimension of the Dead, or, as it is often known, the astral plane." Suddenly, before their eyes, Robin Hood disappeared. The friends looked at each other and then at Ada Lovelace and before she could say anything, as abruptly as he vanished, the archer was back, walking towards them and standing next to the scientist.

Ada Lovelace began pacing again, hands behind her back, returning to lecture mode. "Now, while they are fresh in your minds, put the two concepts you have seen together: the idea that there are other parallel universes creating a multiverse and the thought that one parallel universe is inhabited by the dead. If you trust Robin Hood and I, we can give you details to solidify this theory. We can tell you that when we died, we entered the astral plane – a parallel dimension – known to us as the Otherworld. Robin can then tell you that when he returned as a protector to Sherwood Forest, he crossed back over to Earth from the astral plane. And just now, Robin stepped from our planet into the afterlife and then came back again. If you gave his physical coordinates to someone as he did this, they would not have changed. If you gave the time to someone, it would not have changed. Only one thing really changed – the dimension he was in. Yes, my friends, your leader is a dimension traveller!"

Three

Robin Hood gave his team a break. They stretched their legs, taking a lap of the enclosure and then their leader walked over to a tree, picked up his staff and beckoned them all to come together again by the logs. "These are a lot of details to take in at one time. But, now, let me get to your original question: 'What task do I have for you?' Tell me, what is the biggest challenge on Earth now?"

In unison, the friends said, "Climate change!"

"Exactly. And environmental destruction is not just a modern concept. Did you know that I was one of the first climate activists in history? When we made our home in Sherwood Forest, my men and I, we did so, not only because it was a good hiding place, but because one part of our mission was to protect the great woodland. Many of the poorest families relied on Sherwood for survival. They relied on it for food: hunting wild boar and deer and harvesting roots and plants for vegetables. They used herbs and spices for flavouring and herbs and leaves for medicine; and, of course, they used skins and furs to keep warm during the day and at night. Men and women used branches and brush to build and make fires and, occasionally, chopped down an aging tree or ones that had fallen because of a storm. They used the forest in a sustainable way because they knew their very existence was dependent on the trees. The rich did not care about the longevity of the forest. As always, they thought the world was there for their own personal enjoyment and advancement. They were greedy and destroyed more than they used. I robbed the rich to feed the poor, but I also harassed the rich to keep them out of Sherwood Forest."

As the ghost told his story, the friends were able to listen and place it alongside the many legendary accounts they had heard and read about Robin Hood's life. He had always been associated with the forest, living and hiding in the wild. He had many comrades who lived with him in the forest – a whole band – and he stole from the rich to give to the poor. He was a man of the people and kings and sheriffs hated him. He seemed like a man who would fight for the planet and one they would gladly fight alongside for the planet.

Robin Hood twirled his staff and then knelt, looking into the eyes of each of the friends. "Every one of you has already shown the resiliency and strength we expected, just absorbing all these new experiences over the last few weeks. I want to make sure you understand, each of you will be vital if we are to succeed on this quest. Let me show you one final thing." The ghost took his wooden staff and laid it in the middle of the circle. As the friends leaned in to look, they noticed inscriptions along the length of the brown pole. They, then, heard a metallic swoosh and watched as Robin Hood drew his sword from the leather scabbard that hung from his hip and placed it on the ground alongside the staff.

"Historical artefacts. While one is shiny metal and one smooth wood, both are unique and special. Here are two reasons why Loxley Chase is still strong."

James and Emma both stared, thinking the same thing, then paused and looked at Robin Hood. The ghost nodded and James grasped the middle of the wooden staff as Emma took hold of the hilt of the sword. They stood, lifting the artefacts with them as their friends crowded closer to watch and touch. But, as quickly as they crowded, everyone hopped back, startled by sudden exclamations from James and Emma who dropped the two weapons quickly.

"What did you feel?" Robin Hood had a broad smile on his face.

"The sword was vibrating or something." Emma spoke first and then her brother nodded.

"The staff had power coming from it." James stooped and picked up the long stick again, but, this time, he held on tight and encouraged his sister to do the same with the sword.

"Yes. Power, indeed." Robin Hood gestured for all the group to stand closer again and then he spoke softly. "You have felt the power of Loxley Wood over the last few days and have used it to build your strength and hone your skills. Many thousands of years ago, mankind was more in touch with the earth as a whole – in tune with all the natural world. They recognised that our planet was a living thing, and this understanding helped people to live in harmony with nature – physically and spiritually."

The ghost reached out to James who passed along the staff. Robin Hood positioned it in the centre of the group, gripping it vertically with both hands and then he closed his eyes. Suddenly, all the friends could hear a gentle hum and also could feel a pulsing power coming from the pole.

"There was a time, still thousands of years ago, when our elders sensed that, one day, their world would be in peril, and it would be a peril caused by mankind itself. So, even though these elders were individuals who lived in different regions of the world, in unison, they created vessels to store and concentrate the essence of the earth. These were druids and witches, shamans and priestesses – revered and feared individuals because in the past our planet's power, and the use of that power, was considered magic and only a chosen few could wield it."

"The reason Loxley Wood still exists when forests around the world have died is because we have been guardians of two of these magic vessels for years, along with a living vessel – the Major Oak. It was the mighty Merlin himself who made this sword – Excalibur – into a carrier of the earth's power and thus an enchanted weapon of great renown. And it was Merlin who planted the Major Oak many hundreds of years ago. The earth's power is strong here, so the trees, plants and animals are protected from the effects of climate change – and by extension, the Island of Britain is less ravaged than most. There are more vessels – I know of four objects and four more trees – and each was designed to protect natural areas around the world during the Earth's peril, until that danger could be understood and eradicated. Unfortunately, the peril we now face does not just come in the form of climate change."

Ada Lovelace spoke up again. "I mentioned a parallel world for the dead. The astral plane is for the most part serene and simple – a perfect place for peaceful reflection. But, as greed existed in life, so it does in death and some of the inhabitants of the Otherworld covet the beauty and vitality that is their former home – planet Earth. That is why your name is so perfect: the Pachamama Protectors. We have known for centuries that the Earth needed saving from our own foolishness, from the actions that caused climate change. Only more recently have we understood that there are individuals in the Otherworld who have considered planetary piracy."

The scientist stopped talking and a grave look appeared on her face. She turned to Robin Hood who looked equally sombre as he spoke. "The magic vessels have saved the Earth, but there are spiritual pirates who believe that if they can steal them, they will invigorate the dark reaches of their own world. Unfortunately, we have underestimated the magnitude of this danger. We now know that two vessels have been taken already, both thefts coinciding with the acceleration of climate change on Earth. The task we have for you now is more than protection. We need to safeguard the remaining vessels, but also travel to the Otherworld to regain those that have been stolen."

Homework Assignment One

The revelations shared that day were disturbing and overwhelming, so Robin Hood suggested the friends go home to rest and contemplate. He wanted them to think hard about participating in the quest ahead, a quest which was important but now – with an added journey into the afterlife needed to save the world – was even more dangerous. Their leader made it clear it was okay to say no. Richard, Billy, Mabel and Leah certainly seemed shell-shocked as they left, so much so that they did not see Robin Hood indicating to James and Emma to wait behind.

For the brother and sister, the situation was personal and Robin Hood was aware of that. "I have asked you both for your help but know that you carry a burden that may prevent you from giving everything to our mission. Here, take my staff and visit your father just for a few hours and then bring it back to me tomorrow. I think it will help sustain him over the coming weeks and will give us time to complete our task."

James and Emma did not hesitate and hurried out of the trees, taking turns to carry the unique gift they had been given. They twirled it around like Gandalf in 'Lord of the Rings' or wielded it like a light sabre in 'Star Wars', or both just held it, feeling a warm pulsing in their hands – stunned that they were carrying something that belonged to

Robin Hood. The magic staff must have had its own effect on them, because for thirty minutes they were lost in fantasies, determined to take advantage of the fact that they were in possession of an enchanted tool that was thousands of years old. And then reality and hope hit them when they reached the hospital.

Their father was sleeping and looked pale and small in the bed when they walked into his room. Normally, they would have left him to rest but the brother and sister were too nervous and excited, so Emma gently tapped her dad on the shoulder until he woke up.

"Hey, you two. What a surprise." His voice was groggy from sleep and he stayed in a prone position, head back on the pillow while he gathered his wits. There was a little wince of pain that James and Emma noticed as he tried to adjust his position.

"Sorry to barge in, Dad, but we were too excited to wait. We are, ummmm…" They had not had time to think of a story so James tried to make something up quickly. "We are both working on a project for school. It's kind of a history play and this is one of the props."

Emma laid the old cane on the bed, gently positioning it next to her father's right arm. He slowly looked down at first and then sat up with interest and a little spurt of energy. "Wow, look at that. A staff, and it looks ancient, although I'm sure it's just a replica." Pulling himself into an even more comfortable sitting position, he ran his hands up and down the pole, taking in the worn but polished feel of the wood and the inscriptions. "This looks like Middle English. Interesting. A medieval staff. I can't wait to hear more about this play."

So, James and Emma sat for the next hour, making up a lot of details about a very fictitious play and school project, watching with amazement as the colour came back to their father's cheeks and his voice gained strength. When they finally left, he was sitting with a pad and paper in his lap, making notes about historical characters and events that he thought might help with the project.

That night, the brother and sister hardly slept at all. James set up a sleeping bag on Emma's floor so that they could both be in the same room as the staff, and both were convinced that they could feel gentle waves of warmth rolling out from the wooden pole. In the morning, the children smiled when their mother reported the best night's sleep she had had in months.

When they met in Loxley Wood again, James and Emma explained to their friends what Robin Hood had done to help their father and described the story they had made up so that bringing a stick into the hospital room didn't seem strange.

The ghost nodded appreciatively. "The idea of a fictitious play fits in well with our preparations for the quest. As a group, your next steps are to find out information on certain figures from the past. Each of you will be closely linked to the person I tell you about. They will be important to you, and you to them when we set out on our mission. You can help each other with your research, but you should also focus on the person assigned to you – some of whom are well known, and some not. James, I want you to report back to us on King Arthur; and, Emma, you will take Hua Mulan. Billy, please investigate Hongi Hika. Leah, find out more about Ada

Lovelace. Mabel, look for information on Gouyen; and, Richard, do a report on Hippocrates."

When he had finished giving them their assignments, Robin Hood stood. "I have enjoyed being with you over the last few months. I think I chose well with Emma and James and they, in turn, chose well with their friends. Next week, when we meet, we will continue to practice, but also begin to make a serious plan." Not waiting for any comment, the ghost turned, walked towards the trees and drifted through them and away, leaving the group standing alone together.

"Can you believe we were just given homework by a ghost?" Leah was only half-joking as she turned to follow Emma onto the trail and out of the wood.

Two

Before they all split up and went to their own homes, Emma asked everyone if they would let her father help with the assignments. "He is sick, and along with the cancer, I think he feels hopeless and useless. The look on his face when he thought he might be helping us—it was the happiest I had seen him in a long time. The staff has given him some energy so this 'school play' might help keep his spirits up." The friends all agreed; and so, a few days later, after they'd all managed to google their respective characters, six teenagers paraded into the Sheffield Cancer Centre and chairs were found so that they could all sit around Mr Trueman's bed. He was still very pale and thin but the smile that Emma and James saw on his face was as genuine as they had seen it in a long while, and the brother and sister thought once again about the magic staff and how lucky they were to have met Robin Hood.

"You can't imagine how curious I am about this 'assignment'. Emma tells me you are writing a play and it has an array of historical characters in it. I must say, my wife and I have been out of school for a while but this is a very interesting project. Who was the teacher that set this?"

"It was Mr Archer. He just started in the English Department." Billy's answer was met with rolled eyes from his peers, but James and Emma's dad did not seem to notice anything.

"Okay. If you could tell me about your characters one at a time—but do me a favour. I see you each have some details written down. Put the papers away. Some of the most interesting facts and figures from the past have come from oral history – stories that have been told and retold. I think you should join this tradition. Just tell me what you have discovered, what you remember, in your own words."

James nodded and agreed to go first, putting his sheet of paper on the bed before clearing his throat. "My character is Arthur. He was abandoned by his parents and brought up by the wizard Merlin. Even though he was still a child, he pulled the magic sword 'Excalibur' from a stone when no one else could, revealing himself to be the true King of Britain. Crowned at the age of fifteen, his time in power coincided with an age when Britain was divided, with all of its leaders fighting against each other, and its borders undefended. Even though the odds were against him, he was seen as a successful ruler. He united many lords who had been old enemies and convinced them to fight the Saxons who were constantly crossing the channel from Europe. Even as he fought constantly to bring peace to Britain, as well as keeping invaders at bay, he still found time to launch the legendary search for the Holy Grail.

"Disaster eventually struck his kingdom in the shape of a rebellion raised by Mordred, his nephew. A great battle was fought, nearly all the Knights of the Round Table slain, and Arthur himself was badly wounded."

As James finished and looked up, he noticed that his

father was dozing in his bed, so he whispered quietly, "Is my guy real or made up?"

Leah nodded wisely, indicating that James had been clever to spot the holes in Arthur's history. "I've read that he's made up, that there aren't many mentions of Arthur in real history books, just in poems and stories."

"Remember what Robin Hood said though. Sometimes, if people don't like the figure involved, if he was a rebel in some way, they begin to spread lies and pretend that he didn't exist. Robin Hood is supposed to be mythical and we just sat with him in Loxley Chase." Emma had always enjoyed the tales of King Arthur and the Knights of the Round Table and felt it was her duty to defend him.

Billy cleared his throat and asked if he could go next. Everyone looked at Mr Trueman snoring lightly in the bed, but Emma nodded so Billy put his paper aside, closed his eyes and tried to remember his character.

"Hongi Hika was a Māori war leader who was renowned for his tactical thinking. He built relationships with invading colonists so that he could get resources from them to help battle rival factions in New Zealand. He traded for weapons and then defeated a rival Māori faction in a series of battles called the Musket Wars. As the key leader on the island, he then worked closely with settlers to understand their religious beliefs while also sharing Māori culture. He was responsible for the native language being committed to paper for the first time and developed a relatively peaceful pact with the British which included him travelling to England to meet the king."

The hospital room was silent for a few minutes after

Billy finished. "I know we didn't necessarily want more homework, but I had never heard of this guy. Imagine a leader who, while under attack from a foreign enemy, considers turning the invasion into a tactical advantage against a domestic enemy! Brilliant! He must have been smart as heck."

Leah stood up to go next. "My subject is Ada Lovelace who, of course, we have met!" The girl quickly shot a glance at Mr Trueman to make sure he wasn't awake and thinking, 'How have they met a two-hundred-year-old woman', but he was still dozing. "She was the daughter of poet Lord Byron, a friend of Charles Dickens but also coworker with Charles Babbage. Pretty well connected, then!" Leah looked up, laughing at her own wit. "Babbage was thought to be the father of the computer. Ada was known for poetical science – combining her love of literature and poetry with her mathematical skills. She was believed to be the first person to hypothesize about the possibilities of a computer beyond just numbers. One of her most famous quotes was, 'The more I study, the more insatiable do I feel my genius for it to be.' I like this woman!"

Emma applauded Leah and then leaned forward, closing her eyes, trying to picture her own character who had also impressed her immensely. "As a young woman, Hua Mulan disguised herself so that she could be conscripted into the Chinese Army, taking her ageing father's place. China was under attack from a neighbouring country and Hua Mulan distinguished herself as a fighter for many years, winning the respect of all her fellow soldiers. When she was eventually awarded a medal and a promotion, she revealed herself to be a woman and left to return home to her village as a hero."

Mabel followed Emma's example, closing her eyes to concentrate. "My subject is called Gouyen and, like Billy, I had never heard of her before we got this homework. Gouyen was a member of the Apache tribe and was known for her amazing bravery and heroism. Her first husband was brutally killed in a raid by the rival Comanches and Gouyen took revenge by tracking the raiders back to their camp, disguising herself, luring the Comanche Chief away and then killing him." Mabel opened her eyes and looked at her friends, clearly impressed but in awe of this ferocious young woman from the past. "As the Apache were hunted into extinction by American and Mexican soldiers, Gouyen was as important a warrior to her people as any man in the tribe."

Richard was nodding appreciatively at Mabel when he stood to talk about the final historical figure. "Hippocrates was born in around 460 BC on the Greek Island of Kos. He became known as the father of medicine because even though he lived in ancient times, he brought a lot of modern thought to the science. He was the first person to propose that diseases and illnesses had natural causes and did not occur because of evil spirits or curses. Today, new doctors still say the Hippocratic Oath before they start practicing, pledging upon 'a number of healing gods to uphold ethical standards'."

When everyone had finished reading, they realised that Mr Trueman had fallen into a deeper sleep than before. They all quietly left the room and walked down the stairs and out onto a sunny but chilly street. It was late October and the evenings were getting darker and the winds colder as winter approached. The friends huddled tighter in their coats as they discussed their various historical figures and the new things they had learned about each person. Now the question was, how was this information relevant to the task Robin Hood had for them?

"Hey, do you realise what the date will be next Sunday when we go back to the wood?" Billy didn't wait for an answer. "It's October 31 – Halloween!"

Three

Emma and James tried to keep busy and distract each other as they waited for the weekend and the chance to visit Loxley Chase on such a special night. Their mother always answered the door to trick-or-treaters and liked to put up interesting cultural Halloween decorations for the occasion. This year was obviously a little harder for her, so they helped put out colourful ornaments in the garden and hangings on the door and windows, along with small bowls of sugar skulls for the children. Television, radio and every online gathering place was filled with horror stories and fictional ghouls, but, they, of course, would be spending the evening with a real ghost, so they felt like they had one-upped the world! Was October 31 any different of a night for real ghosts? The protectors discussed this between classes or when walking home from school. In the end, they wanted to ask Robin Hood about Halloween as much as they wanted to tell him about their assigned characters. They also, of course, wanted to discover more about the adventure they were about to undertake.

But, the days dragged, and their lessons were long and their other schoolmates talked about the most tedious things. Finally, Mabel came up with an inspirational idea that took their minds off how slow time was moving. She suggested that they go to the wood in costume and that their costumes be linked to the historical figures they had been assigned. Mabel was delighted to see the excited reaction from the group and more than pleased to help with any sewing and patching that was needed as old clothes were discovered and altered and props made and painted.

When Halloween night came and the Pachamama Protectors walked down the high street in costume, they, of course, were not alone. They were some of the oldest trick-or-treaters out that night, but still blended in with the fun and since they weren't stopping for candy, soon they left all the parents and children behind. All was quiet as usual on Loxley Hill, in the shadow of the wood, and the friends were quiet too. The costume making had been more serious than expected as they tried to be respectful of the periods and cultures they were representing. Leah was wearing a dress from her grandmother's closet to get as Victorian a look as she could, and Mabel had on one of her dad's old brown rugby shirts with a cord tied around her waist to become a resourceful outdoors woman and warrior. James wore all grey to mimic a knight's armour and Emma had found one of her mother's red silk dressing gowns and added a green sash around the middle to create the colour she thought a Chinese warrior might like. Richard had taken the easy route to become a Greek scientist and had just wrapped himself in an old bed sheet; and Billy, thinking of the Māoris who performed traditional dances before rugby matches, had put black and red paint on his face.

When they reached the outskirts of the trees, the friends paused and took deep breaths, as they did every time they came to Loxley Chase. It had been many months since that first-ever visit, but the old wood had not lost any of its darkness, its sinister nature and they were always hushed when they first crossed the boundary from open air to enclosed, whispering silence. Only when they eventually made the clearing and found Robin Hood waiting for them did their excitement overflow. Now, they realised that one of the reasons why the costume idea was so good was that it helped them impress the ghost, allowed him to see how seriously they had taken their assignments. And he was impressed, making them each parade around the outskirts of the glade. As they did this, the aura in the old forest – the magic that Robin Hood had revealed – asserted itself like an invisible mist. James' grey clothes attained the look of real chain metal, Emma's robe shone like a Samurai kimono, Leah's old dress became a Victorian gown, Mabel's rugby shirt looked and felt like a buckskin dress, Richard found himself wrapped in a flowing Greek toga and Billy's face became covered in intricate war paint decorations.

Reciting the history they had learned to Robin Hood now became even more meaningful and they each took turns, immersing themselves in their characters as they spoke. When the last presentation had been made, the friends stared hopefully at the spectre and were rewarded with a broad smile and a nodding head.

"You have all worked hard and it sounds and looks like you have learned about and understand the people from the past that were chosen. That is good. There is a reason you need to understand them. But before we talk about the mission ahead, I have a treat. It was not an accident that you came here on Halloween night. In the old days, we called it Samhain or the festival of the dead. We would put out gifts of food and drink for those that had died so they would be happy and content for another year and would leave the living in peace. Come, let us walk out to the edge of the wood to look down at the village for a while. You are in for a surprise, one that no living person has seen before."

The group were hushed as they followed Robin out and along the trail, back the way they had come, whispering as they walked. 'What had he meant, saying that no living person had seen what they were about to see? What could possibly be in their village that could only be seen by dead people?' Eventually, they all came to the edge of the wood and looked down at the houses and each of the friends present stood in shocked silence, staring at the scene on display. The village of Loxley, as well as being full of children and parents walking around in costumes looking for treats and sweets, was also full of ghosts. Glowing, white and silver spectres mingled with people and glided through the air and down streets, moving in and out of buildings, through open doors and closed walls. They floated and flew above the village, and, from a distance, Loxley glittered and shone like the night sky above as it was overrun with ghosts – more ghosts than people – though the people were completely unaware of what was happening around them.

"This used to happen in cities, towns and villages all over Britain but as the past has been bulldozed and trees and fields ploughed under, so the dead have lost their connection with the living. There is power in the earth as you know, but there is also power in the history, culture, stories of mankind. All life on planet Earth is interwoven, but it is unravelling in so many ways. Loxley is different and it is different because of this old wood. This is all that remains of the great Sherwood Forest and small as it is, it has mystical strength. The dead leave the astral plane and gravitate here once a year because of that – to look, feel, float in that potency and remember the joy that came with living." Robin Hood stopped speaking for a while to allow everyone to watch and wonder at the sight below. Sometimes, the ghosts would fly close to their hill so the children could make out the details of a man or woman, old or young, farmer or sailor, milkmaid or cook, accountant or plumber. The dead, it seemed, came in all shapes and sizes from every period in history; and, for one amazing night, they flew together and remembered together.

"You mentioned joy, Robin Hood. Do the dead feel joy? Or is that left behind when they leave their physical forms?" Emma couldn't take her eyes off the scene below and asked the question quietly.

"Joy may not be the right word, Emma. But do not underestimate peace. Many who die gain harmony in reflection and feel a calmness that comes with not needing to strive any more. Your father – if he leaves us – I know, will be in that place. He has done good things, brought happiness to many and, of course, has raised a good family. When your father dies, he will be at peace in the Otherworld. For others, this takes time. They miss their lives, the energy of the living and the power of planet Earth. Samhain recharges them, helps them continue the process that needs to be followed in death. But I must also be honest, Emma; there is some fear among the dead. They can sense that the world is suffering, that the great trees and oceans and animals that they knew are disappearing. They know that darkness threatens the Earth and so they also come to pay tribute and remember how things were when they were alive. Your quest involves keeping the darkness at bay, and, look, here come some friends who can help."

If the children had been shocked before, when they first came out of the trees to see their village full of phantoms, then they were doubly shocked now as some of those phantoms began to walk up the hill towards them. It was, of course, unbelievable enough that they were standing on a hill with a ghost, watching ghosts, discussing ghosts, but belief was about to be stretched even further. Some of the approaching spirits they recognised, some they didn't, but instinctively they knew who all these ghosts were. Emma had the presence of mind to imagine what it might be like for someone glancing up at the wood just at that precise moment. They would see a group of children dressed as characters from the past and would see walking towards them the ghosts of those same characters from the past, because up the hill came the shimmering, shining figures of King Arthur, Gouyen, Hippocrates, Ada Lovelace, Hongi Hika and Hua Mulan.

Four

As the young friends sat quietly in the clearing, huddled together on logs, looking up with respectful admiration at the ghosts standing in front of them, they realised once and for all that they were not playing a game. At first, maybe it had been quirky, entering a forbidden wood and finding a long-lost famous character who was a ghost, and, of course, it had been fun learning to be an olden day outlaw, living and fighting in the wood. But they had always been able to leave Loxley Chase and return home to their parents and to school and could talk amongst themselves about what a good time they were having and how lucky they were. Now, though, things had really turned serious. They had just left their village – a village that had been flooded by thousands of ghosts, were sitting in front of seven people who had truly made an impact on the world during their lifetimes, all ghosts, and, to top it all, they were being prepared to embark on a mission to save a dying planet. The situation was surreal.

 Robin Hood could see anxiety on the faces of his team, and he spoke quickly and seriously. "My friends, you look troubled. I hope not too troubled. I have grown to like you and trust you in the last few days and weeks as we have worked together, and I am excited to begin this new phase of our adventure. Of course, to be sitting, surrounded by such figures of consequence from the past is a surprise, but

I think it is a necessary surprise. Necessary, perhaps overdue, because every day that passes now is a day lost. You know these great men and women. They are here because they want to help and we think that they will be the best people to help given your characteristics, the individualities that make up our Pachamama Protectors. But they are also here because of their own characteristics, the skills they had in life and have retained in death – and because of the passion they have for Mother Earth. Now is the time to look inside yourselves, to examine how strong you really are, how passionate you are about your friends, your families, your world. If, at this crucial moment, fear overwhelms that passion, I will respect that, but I will also tell these heroes to leave and I will tell you to leave. It would be hard to start my search again from nothing, to find unique individuals like yourselves who might help me, but if it must be, it must be. You are young and it is perhaps unfair to demand such certainty in youth. But we cannot afford to leave on this mission without absolute conviction."

Emma was about to speak but saw James look her way with raw emotion in his eyes. She knew, out of everyone present, this adventure meant the most to her brother. From the moment they had first stepped foot into Loxley Chase and discovered Robin Hood, James had also discovered hope for the first time – he had finally found a way to fight his father's illness. Though it scared her to think how upset her brother might be if these ghosts and their mission could not ultimately save their dad, still she needed to be supportive. So, she kept quiet and nodded to James and he stood to speak for the group.

It was unusual for his friends to see James hesitate, be unsure of himself. In the past few months, it had seemed like anger might carry him through any situation. But, of course, this was very different. Visibly, James shook himself, took a deep breath and spoke clearly. "Robin, I think we all respect and admire the great people that are here, and no one could question the meaning of our quest. But it is more important to us to have been chosen by you. There aren't many people who can say that they have Robin Hood as a friend so I think we want to carry on and help however we can. Also, on behalf of the living, I think we need to thank these leaders for agreeing to come back and help. And on behalf of myself, Emma, my mum and dad…" James choked up and looked around at his friends, who were smiling and nodding in agreement. Then he sat, and they all looked expectantly up at the assembled spirits.

Robin Hood walked over to the brother and gently placed a hand on his head, then returned to the group of ghosts. "I thank you, James, and I thank all my protectors. Rest assured that we all think you are the right people to help with this mission, that the Earth is in good hands as it tries to survive this unprecedented danger. Soon, we will explain our plan – the details of this quest. You have trained well in your bodies and hearts; now, we need to engage your minds. How tactically do we plan to achieve our aims? But, first, you should formally meet your new teammates. The Pachamama Protectors team has grown. Let us meet your six new members." The archer turned to his fellow ghosts and opened his arms, offering them the floor. It was Gouyen who stepped forward.

Emma and James both quickly looked at each other as

they often did. Because they were brother and sister and so connected, words were not needed to explain their shared emotion. The woman, or ghost of a woman, in front of them was diminutive in size. She looked like what she had been, a mother, wife, caregiver to her family and traditional Apache tribeswoman. But they had heard her story, how ferocious she had been in exacting her revenge on her enemies and they could feel that ferocity in her presence now. It was as if the natural power that Robin Hood had shown them in Sherwood Forest was being channelled by this ghost but was also being matched by her own Native American physical and mystical strength.

And then their guess was shown to be true in a breathtaking way. Gouyen did not speak but held out one hand flat, then blew on the palm. Almost immediately, the friends felt a stream of sensations and emotions enter their minds and bodies. They could tell how close this woman had been to nature, how she had used its gifts – energy, power, history and spirituality to enrich and heal her own friends and family. They were aware how painful it was to know that the Earth was dying and how ardently she wanted to help save it. Before she left, several of the forest's spiritual animals came walking out of the trees to join her. A deer, a badger and a beautiful grey wolf. Then, without a word, they all walked slowly away.

Next, Hua Mulan took centre stage. The youngsters had barely come to terms with 'meeting' Gouyen when a new presence announced itself to their senses. The Chinese warrior had long black hair that flowed along her shoulders and beautiful, smooth skin. She also had a lethal samurai sword hanging from her waist and her own aura of strength and determination that pulsed into the group. The feeling she exuded did not exclude the importance of saving the Earth but was focused more on achieving victory in battle. This was a tough lady. She demonstrated that toughness by drawing her sword and performing a balletic, but military dance in front of them, waving and thrusting her blade, sliding and kicking her feet, finishing with a standing somersault and a single chanted word, 'Xièxiè'.

Such a unique set of introductions and the excitement at Hua Mulan's display intertwined nicely with the tingling feeling all the protectors still felt from Gouyen. Then, it was Ada Lovelace's turn. She did not move, just winked and waved. "We've met."

There was laughter; and, then, a much more enigmatic figure stepped forward: one who had been intriguing them all since the day he was assigned to Billy as a research subject. Hongi Hika's aura was peaceful but also the most complex of all the ghosts. It felt like there were layers of belief, knowledge and intent standing in front of them. Whereas the dominant feeling from Gouyen was love and respect for Mother Nature and from Hua Mulan, strength and a passion for victory, Hongi Hika had many sensations that drifted from him. A thought entered each of the young minds at the same time. *It's like the aroma from a bubbling stew.*

All eyes were drawn to the intricate artwork that covered the Māori warrior's face and neck – beautiful, meaningful tattoos; and then he extended both palms towards the friends and as they watched, small beads of light popped out, like little bubbles from a fish undersea. These bubbles then floated in the air, six at one time and drifted towards each individual. Mabel put her hand out and a bubble landed and then disintegrated on her skin. She inhaled sharply because it felt like a small water balloon had popped, leaving a warm sensation that flowed down her fingers and up her arm, eventually bathing her body in pulsing, gentle heat. The other friends followed Mabel's lead and for a few minutes, each of them was standing, eyes closed, feeling, smelling and hearing a faraway island with tall snowy mountains, deep blue lakes, green valleys and waves crashing noisily onto sandy shores. Before he left, Hongi Hika stared at each child and they realised they could now see colour in the ghost, and ghosts. His face tattoos were intricate reds and blues and over to the side, Robin Hood's clothing was now a rich forest green.

The protectors were left for a few minutes to enjoy the gifts they had received, visual and sensual; and, then, Hippocrates came forward and indicated that they should sit cross-legged in a circle, holding hands. They closed their eyes and the Greek physician hummed and then sang a soft soothing chant. Almost immediately, each person began to see images in their minds. They could sense that it was a shared vision through the squeezing of each partner's hand in the circle but it was not a frightening daydream in any way, so they all relaxed and concentrated on the experience. It was a story told in pictures and words, with Hippocrates' chant changing to a melodic narration.

'Derfel curled up in a tight ball to make sure he was as hidden as possible in the thick ferns that lined the trail. A battle raged around him with voices raised in anger,

shouting and yelling in a strange language. A horse reared and landed, hooves inches from his hiding place and then a knight fell, badly wounded, armour clanking as it hit the ground. The noises were frightening and deafening and Derfel risked causing the ferns to move, risked revealing his hiding place, because he had to bring his hands up flat against his ears, to try and muffle the sounds of clashing swords and screams of pain. It seemed like he was in hiding for hours as the fighting continued on and on, but still he remained motionless. Fear had silenced the ache of his own muscles, muscles that had been clenched and curled in one place for too long, but that agony was released at last when there was finally calm in the glade surrounding his hiding place. When Derfel crawled out from under a bush, from behind his ferns, he had to take a moment to stretch and bend before he ran from the misery of that battlefield.

The boy had been travelling for weeks and those weeks had been full of hidden danger. It was not safe to travel in Europe alone, especially when you were healthy and strong and English. The capture of slaves was common and an English slave would be a trophy in Germany or France, but Derfel had no choice but to place himself in danger because he needed to get back home. He needed to talk to his king, to tell Arthur where he had been and what he had seen. He needed to tell Arthur that his friend, Arthur's closest friend, was dead, that he, Derfel, had witnessed the fall of Galahad and that he also knew where the hiding place was. He needed to tell him all of these things, except Arthur was hundreds of miles away and he was just a thirteen-year-old boy in a strange, foreign land

– alone.

But his master and mentor Galahad had taught him well and if he had been asked, he would have admitted that, even though for days he had been sad and scared, once he had recovered his wits, his journey had been exciting and liberating. After his escape, he had stolen a horse from a barn and had ridden for days, with the sun at his back during the morning and in his face during the evening. Always go west, Galahad had said, and that was what he was doing. The horse was a good one, young and brown with white speckles, and he was a good rider so they covered ground quickly. It was not hard to stay hidden in the forests of Europe. He had thought that nowhere could be as beautiful as Britain, as green and fragrant as his homeland, but as he travelled along trails and riverbanks, he grew to appreciate the trees and plants and animals that existed in an enemy land. When he heard or saw people in the distance, he would jump off his horse and would lead her around a travelling convoy, or maybe a small village or town. At night, he would tie up his mount and forage for roots and berries and sometimes sneak onto farms to takes eggs from chicken hatches or apples from an orchard. He had been resourceful and careful because he wanted to continue enjoying his freedom, and he was afraid of the consequences of getting caught, but most of all because he wanted to make it back home, to deliver his message for Galahad, for Arthur and for England. And then he had blundered into a battle. He should have, would have heard fighting except, it had not started when he had arrived. Enemies were sneaking up on each other and by the time he had seen warriors appear and been frightened by their bellowing, attacking cries, it had been too late. Luckily, the warring tribes had been intent on each other, and so, as quickly as possible, he had jumped from his horse and scampered into the undergrowth to hide and hope. His horse had galloped away, fighting had boiled up around him and when peace returned, he was on foot. But, at least, he was deep into the countryside of France, he was sure of that. Galahad had whispered into his ear as they had journeyed together on a different, bigger horse, arms tied tightly together, guards on either side. He had whispered a map, a route, special landmarks and signs to look out for that he could use if he were to escape. And escape he had. Mordred had made a mistake; after killing Galahad, he had wanted to gloat in front of at least one prisoner and so he had left the boy alive and he had opened the container too soon. But, not too soon for Derfel, and so he had run and run, faster than he had ever run in his life although a bright light and a feeling of goodness and hope had been trying to pull him back.

He had run and ridden and now he was in France and close to the coastline. He was confident because one of the landmarks Galahad had told him about had been the cathedral at Reims, a towering church that was a renowned place of worship for the French. Derfel had passed that, had ridden wide and around the church and the town of Reims just before he had blundered into the battle, so he thought he was maybe one hundred miles from the beaches of Calais and then a short crossing by boat to the safety of Britain.

It was a powerful thought, to know he was so near after so long, and so he walked and ran a little, grinding out the miles, getting closer and closer after a gruelling journey. Even though he badly wanted to get home, could almost taste his mother's cooking, still he continued to admire the countryside of France. Galahad had named a variety of trees as they had ridden, bound together, had nodded to pines and poplars and beech trees. He saw them again on his long walk to Calais, as they waved around in warm breezes, their branches housing hawks and falcons along with common thrushes and magpies. In the mornings, while Derfel was still stretching out his body after a night under a blanket of leaves, he saw rabbits and badgers scampering in the dew-covered grass or otters and beavers sniffing and searching around on riverbanks. The surroundings were peaceful and picturesque and for a boy who had been used to hard work and following orders, cleaning and cooking and carrying weapons for his masters, the freedom that came with his message-carrying quest could not be ignored – it needed to be enjoyed because it could be gone in a flash. If he was not careful, he could still be captured by the French and, of course, once he was home and had delivered his message, he would return to the chores he had known all of his life, before he had been captured with his master, had been taken with Galahad on a journey around the world and back.

Derfel eventually stole another horse, an older and weaker one this time, but still it helped him make it to the coast in good time. Once in the dockyards of France, he knew he had to reveal himself, had no trees to hide in, and so he looked for the right person quickly. Galahad had told him that it was traditional for fishermen of all nationalities to mingle, that they all worked in the same seas and caught the same fish and so rivalries were not as common as they were for regular folk. Still, there were allegiances and so Galahad had given him a small piece of paper with Arthur's seal on it, stamped in wax. He had told him to watch, listen and hope that when he found a fisherman from England, it would be a fisherman that was good and loyal to his king. When Derfel spotted a strong young man with long brown hair and a smile full of teeth, loading his ship and talking to colleagues in English, he approached him and knew immediately that he had been lucky. The captain ruffled his hair, looked both ways down the dock and then ushered him on board to sit in hiding amongst the nets and crab traps on the boat.

Derfel had been at sea only once before, and then he had been back-to-back with Galahad, in ropes again, tied securely to the mast of another fishing boat. On that voyage, he had been violently ill, leaning away from his master and retching onto the deck, comforted only by the soothing words of his lord. On the return journey, the waters were calmer and perhaps he was older, more experienced because he breathed in the salty air and watched the rolling waves this time with fascination. When they reached the port of Folkestone, Derfel was almost sad to leave the boat. He gave his new friend a handshake and then set off on strong walking legs, close to the end of his journey, a piece of paper now clutched in his hand – a note that had been hidden in his boot in Europe. The paper had two words scrawled on it in Galahad's untidy handwriting, word's intended for one man's eyes only and so Derfel made for the city of the king's, walked in the direction of Winchester and the castle of Camelot.

His walk was not long this time, however. Derfel did not need to make it all the way to Camelot to hear the news of Arthur's death, of the rebellion started by the traitor Mordred that had killed Britain's last chance. He did not need to make it all the way to Winchester to sense the feelings of despair in the air, to know that the Saxon armies were free to run wild through Britain now that the strength and power of Arthur had been removed. Derfel thought back to the hope that had kept Galahad strong, that had sustained his lord until the end and then the messenger sat and cried like the thirteen-year-old boy he was. He had been tough, had carried his note far, but now he needed his father, his mother, wanted the security of a home he had left many years ago when he had been found and chosen to be a servant of knights. He needed his parents again and so he set off on foot once more, heading north instead of west, heading for Yorkshire. Quickly, he reached the boundaries of Sherwood Forest and began to feel better. After a few miles walking in the shade of strong, sturdy oaks, he realised one thing he had learned, that the green countryside of Germany and France had been unexpected and nice, that he had not imagined the fields and woods in a foreign land could compare to English nature. They would be okay. This was England and another king would come, another hero would emerge to keep them safe and free, Derfel was sure of that. He spotted a deer ahead and ran after it at full speed, laughing out loud because he was happy. He may have failed to deliver his message, but, at least, he was home.'

When the dream was over, a rich, engaging voice

asked them to open their eyes. The friends did so and shuffled their positions so they were all looking up at a figure that seemed, in aura and presence, to be the equal of Robin Hood. He was dressed a little like the archer except not in green – with loose leggings tucked into sturdy boots, a grey shirt and cloak and a sandy blond beard and shoulder length hair. He was also wearing Excalibur on his hip. The sword had been returned to its rightful owner. His eyes were deep blue and piercing, and his gaze went from one friend to another in turn before he spoke again.

"The legendary Pachamama Protectors. Young but already legendary in the Otherworld." Everyone gaped, amazed at being called legendary by King Arthur. "We all thank you for agreeing to help us because this is no small task. Robin Hood has explained that two containers, holders of Mother Earth's power, are missing. That is another quest that we will embark on soon, with your help. Our friends, Gouyen and Hongi Hika, have vessels in their homelands – one in the branches of an old kauri tree in New Zealand and one buried next to a giant redwood in California. Both artefacts are safe for the time being. But one last vessel, a special container, is under threat as we speak. It is the one that you just heard about from brave Derfel. My friends, our task now is to travel to Europe, to find and secure the grail itself."

Companions
One

If the days before Halloween had passed by slowly then the days after—after they had learned the truth about the quest and a date had been set to leave, those days flew by in a blur. Of course, they had homes and parents and school and all the normal things they had to do and places they had to go, but now they were seekers of the grail and normal life was not normal any more. They had to double the times they visited Loxley Chase because they needed to practice their combat skills and sit with legends to talk and listen and understand more about lives that were well known on the surface but not so well known underneath the surface. Robin Hood was adamant that if they were to be successful as a team then they needed to understand each other as a team, not just superficially, and so deep conversations were held.

Emma was fascinated by Hua Mulan and the warrior, amazingly, reciprocated those feelings. She was deeply interested in Emma's Asian Indian heritage and her reflections on being adopted and growing up in a foreign land. Emma was honest about her experiences: awkward at times because her skin colour was different and she felt like an outsider; more ingrained emotional loneliness, perhaps, because she felt culturally unique in her surroundings, although she arrived as a very young child.

But she could not have had more caring parents, or a more steadfast and supportive brother and Loxley Chase seemed to wrap its arms around her; it was such a special place. Which meant most of her reflections were positive.

Hua Mulan, in turn, talked about growing up in a feudal society dominated by the ruling class and men. She talked about the hidden fury she felt, because she was stronger, faster and cleverer than most boys in her village but could never fully utilise these skills. She also talked about the poverty she experienced and the sadness she felt for her mother and father who worked so hard. Those were the areas where they felt a deep connection: gender irrelevance, woman power and a love of family.

Richard also found a surprising amount in common with Hippocrates. They, too, both had caring parents, although Richard's suffered from ill health while the Greek physician's mother and father had been strong. Hippocrates' father had been a doctor and so he spent a lot of time guiding and supporting his son as he looked to follow in his dad's footsteps. What really struck Richard was that, while his ghostly companion had grown up in a wealthy household, Hippocrates did not take a safe path and stick to the accepted norms and rules in medicine at that time. He truly wanted to help people and so investigated, experimented and fundamentally changed a lot about medicine in his day. Hippocrates encouraged Richard to think along those lines too when it came to becoming a doctor but also in everyday life. He pointed out that Richard's participation as a Pachamama Protector was very brave – certainly not taking the easy option in life – and he was very proud of him and proud to be his partner on this adventure.

Leah found her one-on-one with Ada Lovelace easy because they had already connected in a profound way and were so similar in their outlooks. When the ghost had been describing the scientific aspects of their quest and had called Leah her assistant, she had immediately forged a tight bond with the young girl. Now, all they did was talk about science and mathematics and Leah peppered her companion with questions about her work, Einstein, parallel dimensions and if the dimension of the dead was actually a theory and, if so, had it been developed on paper, with facts and figures?

Probably the most intense and impactful conversation that occurred between companion and protector was when Gouyen and Mabel met up in secret early one morning, on the opposite side of Loxley Wood to their normal meeting place. When they saw each other, Mabel immediately started crying and Gouyen had wrapped her arms around her and comforted her for more than five minutes. They eventually sat beneath a tree and the Apache leader asked about the tears.

"I don't know." Mabel had welled up again briefly but took some deep breaths and then found she could speak. "As soon as Robin Hood gave me your name to investigate, I felt an affinity. It was very strange because, at that point, I didn't know anything about you. Then I did some research, and the feelings went deeper and deeper; and when you showered us with your emotions the other day, at your introduction, I honestly felt like you were my sister. I know you are older than me, but it wasn't a motherly feeling. You were a friend, a soulmate."

Gouyen patted the girl on her knee. "I felt that way about you too. The gifts I gave to you and to your friends were emotional keys to the magic of Isanaklesh. But I gave you a little more, Mabel. Because there will come a time very soon when you will need it. My people were nomads by choice. We moved with the seasons until the invaders forced us to abandon that way of life. Your ancestors had no choice. You were forced to leave your homeland and that experience is deep in your soul, which is why we are sisters. Stay close to me on this quest. We will need each other."

Like Mabel, Billy and James were secretive about their meetings. They broke the rules and had their conversations together. Billy had called James one night from his house and admitted that while he was pleased he had Hongi Hika as his companion, he was very intrigued by King Arthur. When James expressed the same feelings, they agreed to a group meeting and neither boy was disappointed. On the face of it, Arthur was all warrior, wielding Excalibur and bludgeoning his Saxon and Anglo enemies into submission. But then he told stories about travelling to Stonehenge with Merlin and laying on the dew-soaked grass all night to commune with the gods. He also fished out an amulet from his tunic, an iron Norse lucky charm that he always wore into battle.

Hongi Hika seemed to be the opposite of Arthur, very focused on Māori beliefs and cultures, most visible in his ornate face tattoos. But the New Zealand native also had some ferocious tales – attacking enemy tribes and invaders with fleets of war canoes and beheading rival chiefs who refused to submit to his leadership. Billy and James found the conversations with both great leaders blissful.

The friends all met at a tea shop in the village one weekend, without the ghosts, to compare notes about their meetings. It was a fascinating session of sharing for all. Emma finished the discussion with a thought that had been bothering her. "Isn't it strange that we aren't more afraid? I mean we're only kids and we're about to set off God knows where with a bunch of strangers who died hundreds of years ago; and we have to battle whatever thing or things took the other relics. Don't you think we should be afraid?"

Billy had a theory. "I think we are being affected by Loxley Chase – the power that Robin Hood talks about – even more than we know. James, remember the other day when I got into an argument with Steven Wright during that football match against Rotherham Grammar School?" James smiled and thought back to his friend reading the riot act to another midfielder who was not trying hard enough in the game. "I mean I don't like taking charge but just felt like I had to. And it worked! He set me up for the winning goal five minutes later!" Billy's fist pumped up in the air as he described the feeling of winning the game.

Richard nodded his head in agreement. "I am definitely not an athlete, as you all know, but I've recently been thinking a lot more about my health. I mean, I do want to be a doctor after all! I'm not sure if it's the wood influencing me, or just the fact that I don't want to let anyone down on this quest, but I've been walking every morning before breakfast and even visited the school gym the other day."

There was a group moment of silence as they

considered these revelations, and then when Emma asked what else was going on, Leah blushed. "I have to admit I kind of feel... well... humble now and then!" Everyone laughed. "You know Kyle, that loser from first period history—well I actually volunteered to partner up with him on an assignment the other day and he got a B plus. He kissed me on the cheek in front of the whole class!"

"Okay, so we've all become better people because of our visits to Loxley Chase but we've also been bewitched into not worrying about the dangers of this quest. I think we need to keep our wits about us, don't you?" Emma was trying to force her point home, but it wasn't working.

James did not know if he was a better person, but certainly felt like a much calmer person since Halloween; and he answered his sister in this new, thoughtful and peaceful way. "I think that it's good we have you looking out for us, sis, and I agree we should be careful. I think it's a bit strong to say we're bewitched though. Maybe we just believe in what we're doing? Maybe we just believe more in the cause than we do in our own personal safety."

Two

As the quest loomed closer, the friends practiced their drills in Sherwood with a new intensity. This was helped when each of them was given a present by Hua Mulan. "These are called bang staffs. They are traditionally used in Chinese martial arts, but we made them from branches of the Major Oak. They may not seem as strong as a sword but they are. They will help you to channel earth power when you fight."

The increased prowess of the group in combat wasn't a sudden thing. They had been practicing hard, but with the effects of the magical introductory gifts from the ghosts still pulsing through their bodies and new charmed bang staffs to wield, each member of the Pachamama Protectors felt like they really were accomplished fighters. Their weapons were fitted into leather scabbards on their backs, which made them easy to carry and pull out, over their shoulders. When sparring, it was like the staffs were attuned to their senses plus had minds of their own, meaning the intensity level at practices was now off the charts. Mabel and Billy had a fifteen-minute fight when neither of them could break down the other's defences; and when Emma and James went at each other, Hippocrates had to call a halt before someone was hurt.

Each of them also found that having different teachers help with different skills led to even more improvement.

There was no way they would not pay attention when King Arthur pulled out Excalibur to help with a particular defensive practice; Robin Hood was, of course, Robin Hood and so their accuracy with the bow and arrow improved daily; and Hua Mulan was amazingly tough, fighting with her fists and feet, making it quite clear why she had managed to fit in easily as a disguised warrior in the Chinese Army. Then there was Gouyen. She appeared kind, gentle and helpful on the outside but when Robin Hood asked her to demonstrate how to use a knife and, more impressively, how to disarm someone else with a knife, she was brutal and quick.

Robin soon asked the friends to go and see Mr Trueman – to talk about the grail. "Billy, you need to get into a strategy mindset. I think every little detail will help with this mission. Hongi Hika, Gouyen and Hua Mulan are good tacticians, but even they need all the facts at their fingertips to be able to come up with an achievable plan. We know the geographical area where the grail can be found but understanding more about how it got there might help us successfully reclaim it."

Which meant the group made another visit to the hospital, and, once again, James and Emma brought the staff along to lay on their father's bed. It took him a little time to wake up, but his breathing seemed stronger as he lay rubbing his fingers over the inscriptions on the wood. And, again, he seemed to like having the children there, as though it made him feel needed. He really perked up when they asked him to talk about the grail.

"Well, that is a fascinating subject. You boys and girls have certainly taken an interest in some new and exciting topics, haven't you? Is this part of the play you are all doing with Mr Archer?" There was quiet head nodding, then from memory Mr Trueman began to tell them about the legend of the Holy Grail.

"The Holy Grail was a vessel used by Jesus Christ at the Last Supper. It was then given to his grand-uncle, St Joseph of Arimathea. After the crucifixion, Joseph was supposed to have been imprisoned in a rock cave like the one Jesus had been put into after he had died. Left to starve, he was sustained for several years by the power of the grail which provided him with fresh food and drink every morning. Later, St Joseph travelled to Britain with his family and several followers. He settled at what was then called Ynys Witrin but is now called Glastonbury, but the grail was taken to Corbenic where it was housed in a castle.

"Centuries later, the location of the great castle of Corbenic became forgotten. At the court of King Arthur, however, it was told that the grail would one day be rediscovered by a descendant of St Joseph, someone who was the best knight in the land. When such a man arrived in the form of Galahad, the son of Lancelot, the quest to find this holiest of relics began. Through many adventures and many years, the Knights of the Round Table crossed Britain from one end to another in their search. Perceval discovered the castle first but could not find the grail and left empty-handed. Lancelot reached Corbenic next, but he was prevented from entering because he had cheated on his wife and so was not thought to be worthy. Finally, Galahad arrived and he was permitted entry to the Grail Chapel and allowed to gaze upon the great cup. His life became complete and together the grail and man were lifted up to heaven."

It seemed the more they learned about their own quest, the more spectacular and adventurous it became. To think they would be following in the footsteps of the Knights of the Round Table, and, in particular, Lancelot and Galahad! The girls, it seemed, were a little more grounded than the boys, however. They questioned why Perceval couldn't find the cup when he had found the castle, whose business it was what Lancelot did with his wife and that it was unlikely that the grail went up to heaven before ending up in Europe.

"As unlikely as finding half a dozen ghosts in Sherwood Forest, I suppose." James may have been calmer now than in the past, but he could still get upset when the mystery behind this adventure was questioned. Billy decided they should all speak to King Arthur when they next practiced in Loxley Chase. Arthur could add more detail to the story and place it into context alongside Derfel's tale.

A few days later, after a strenuous afternoon of fighting, the friends all gathered around as James repeated Mr Trueman's account of the grail to Arthur. "Your father has told you a good version of the legend. The only questionable part is the ending, of course. Since the grail disappeared, it was romantic to say that Galahad had gone to heaven carrying the cup. Galahad certainly went to the Otherworld because he died soon after his discovery. He was the only man who, without a doubt, held the grail after Joseph of Arimathea, but he was kidnapped somewhere on the road between Corbenic and Camelot with his servant

Derfel. That was the last we saw of the grail apart from rumours and stories that have led people astray ever since."

Billy was having more fun now than at any time in this adventure. Meeting such amazing characters from the past and learning more about them was very interesting. The weapons practice was good exercise and obviously important because of the dangers they might face. But what he really loved to do was solve puzzles and analyse problems to find answers. He felt sure that if they probed harder, King Arthur might remember more of the grail and its journey. After all, he had been there at the time this mystery had taken place. Billy had listened extra hard to Mr Trueman at the hospital, and he had given total concentration to Arthur when he spoke.

Now he probed. "If you had been Mordred, what would have been your plan for the grail, after you had stolen it?"

"Great question, Billy, and exactly the one I have been asking myself. My friends in the Otherworld have been helping me work through some ideas over the last few months. We think it was Joseph of Arimathea who made the grail into a vessel for the earth's essence, perhaps in the time he was locked away in the cave. He was a very holy man and a magician, definitely in touch with the strengths of Mother Earth. We are sure that Mordred captured Galahad after he and the Knights of the Round Table discovered the grail and then used him to carry the vessel as he made his escape. Not everyone can be close to or touch earth power, especially not someone as evil as Mordred. Remember the story of the sword and the stone?

No one could retrieve Excalibur, except Merlin and me. That is even more true of the grail which, of course, also once held the blood of Jesus. It is a powerful artefact – the mightiest of all the vessels."

Arthur continued, stroking his beard as he considered his words, "Mordred was the son of King Uther and next in line for the throne when he died. I was an illegitimate child of Uther, so not a true heir. But Mordred was a wicked, wicked child and then an equally malevolent man so he was destined to only rule for a short time. Merlin always said that evil spirits entered his soul at childbirth and I was eventually forced to believe him after Mordred nearly ruined Britain only two years into his reign. I overthrew him and he never forgave me or my knights for taking away his throne, but he was lucky I did not kill him. It turns out I should have; because not only did he slay Galahad and steal the grail, once he sent the chalice away, he joined forces with the Saxons and led a rebellion against me before rejoining the grail journey."

When Arthur had finished, Ada Lovelace, Hippocrates and Gouyen came and sat in the circle to add their thoughts to the discussion. "We know the grail was taken to Europe after it was stolen." The Greek physician began to talk first. "Because of its extraordinary potency, we know it caused sickness in anyone trying to use it for destruction or greed, while at the same time it nurtured the surrounding landscape. We were able to find many instances of a mysterious plague alongside an unexplained natural growth and abundance that moved across Western Europe and Southern Europe, down into Africa, and then back into Eastern Europe around this time. There are at least two unexplained desert oases that we think are linked to this journey."

Next, Ada Lovelace leaned into the discussion. "There was clearly a long-term, evil plan in place for the grail that began with stealing and hiding it. Mordred and his backers needed to make it safe to transport. We think someone had an idea that certain kinds of heavy metal might be able to block its power. That is why the trail of sickness and growth led into Africa. A strong vein of lead exists there and is only mined near the Congo River. We believe that Mordred's men took Galahad to Africa, forcing him to transport the grail, although its powers still radiated out into the air along the way. Ironsmiths eventually fashioned a container made from Congolese lead, Galahad was murdered and then the grail was taken to a region near the border of Belarus. We think Mordred brought a small force with him to rejoin the grail there, after the rebellion against Arthur. The numbers of deaths and fertile growths were fewer and fewer as the trail moved towards Eastern Europe and we think that was because the container was being finished and hardened as they travelled. But it is our thought that those carrying the grail still underestimated its power. They were exposed for long enough, so even after they had hidden the grail, all the servants of Mordred – and, Mordred himself, we are sure – died and thus the vessel was lost to the outside world."

It was captivating for the children, hearing such famous people aiding them with their planning, each joining in as the mystery was unravelled. There seemed to be very little ego present in the clearing. Perhaps, that was what happened when the whole world was threatened. Or maybe Robin Hood had just chosen his allies well.

Gouyen spoke next. "We have looked through the history books and have spoken to spirits from the past and we have found additional clues to confirm this theory. Clue number one: a Congolese king, Ganga Zumba, talks about his village being home to the mummified figure of a British knight, dating back to the year six or seven hundred, around the time of Arthur and Mordred. We think the tribe was compensated for the lead and also given Galahad's body and armour and over the years the mummy became like a museum piece for other villages to visit and admire. Clue number two: during World War II, Commander Ivan Konev of the Russian Army invaded Poland and he remembers struggling to advance in a region near to Brest, around the Białowieża Forest area, because of the unusual density of trees and undergrowth and because local prisoners and workers would not go near the forest. He investigated and found out that all the inhabitants of that area avoided the forest because of centuries old stories of spirits and ghosts."

"Finally, clue number three, which just speaks to the bravery of young Derfel. Have you ever heard of the York parchment?" Nodding heads all around. It was a very famous historical artefact housed in York cathedral. "It is a small piece of paper that miraculously survived from the seventh century without any sign of age at all. Do you know what the two words were on that parchment? Białowieża Forest."

Robin Hood was sitting on a nearby stump of wood, smoothing the shafts of a set of arrows and he spoke up when the mathematician had finished. "Białowieża lies on the border of Belarus and Poland. Obviously with the parchment as evidence and with the resilience of nature in the region even as climate change took hold, we have long suspected the grail to be hidden in those trees. It is an intriguing part of the world for many reasons. Very little is known about the area because, since it is on the border of Poland and what was Russia, few outsiders have visited. Those two countries have been secretive or at war with their neighbours for many years. That an ancient forest has survived in a highly industrialised and polluted part of the world is no accident. It is a concrete and steel jungle but there sits the Białowieża Forest."

Arthur joined the conversation. "I visited that region once with Mordred when he was young and we were trying to stop invasions of Britain by Saxon and Germanic tribes. The Białowieża Forest was huge, perfect for the tribesmen to hide in. Many times, our knights were ambushed, with hundreds of enemy men surging out from the trees. Our foray into foreign land was not successful, although it may have been for Mordred. I believe that when he was considering stealing and then finding a place to hide the grail, he remembered how dense and thick the trees were in Poland." The king spoke about Mordred – his enemy – with a bitterness that had not been diluted over the centuries.

Billy was still avidly listening to each of the storytellers and now spoke up. "I'm wondering, have you encountered Mordred in the Otherworld?"

Robin Hood gently applauded. "Again, good thinking, Billy. We have not, although we had men and women searching for him. There is reason to believe he is my counterpoint in this region although we have different aims in mind. I am in Sherwood Forest as a guardian of nature. Mordred is in Białowieża as a point man for evil. He waits for his allies so they can once again steal the grail."

Three

Gouyen knelt down in the centre of the clearing and waved her hand over a pile of kindling and branches, starting a blaze to warm the youngsters. Amazingly, it appeared to be smokeless but still had heat. With everything else going on, this did not surprise the friends. They had come to respect and welcome the powers of the ghosts and of Sherwood Forest itself. All of the log chairs present were pulled together and the group sat in a close circle.

Hua Mulan smiled encouragingly. Serious topics were being discussed and she wanted the young members of the team to remain confident. "Protectors, you must have questions."

Leah raised her hand. "Who exactly is the enemy? And you mentioned before two artefacts being stolen. What happened and where were they taken?"

Hongi Hika, who had been quiet for some time, squeezed the young girl's shoulder and said, "Thank you, Leah. We need to bring our planning to a conclusion so you can feel truly prepared. Vessels have already been taken from Africa and South America: a Maasai spear from Kenya and a hunting hatchet, originally made by the Kayapo people, from the Amazon. We think our enemies have plans for North America and New Zealand, but, first, they want the grail. We have been caught off guard while our opponents have been readying themselves for decades.

Be aware that we have discussed this and all involved acknowledge their mistakes and failures. We were victim to age-old cultural, racial and geographical biases. Robin Hood came to Sherwood Forest many years ago in good faith because of his personal affinity with the great forest. But he and we acknowledge there should have been a deeper effort to safeguard other regions. A mighty baobab tree was burned to the ground in Kenya and a truly majestic banyan tree experienced the same fate in Brazil. The stolen vessels are now in the darker realms of the astral plane. One thing I would say is, Robin Hood personally led the recruitment efforts to make sure the team that is now responsible for saving the planet is diverse and globally representative."

Robin Hood looked sad but gave a respectful smile to the Māori for his report, took a deep breath and decided to move on. "There was a second part to your question, Leah – who exactly is the enemy? Maybe that was where our wise ancestors erred in their planning. They foretold the peril that would come to the planet itself. They understood that lust for money and power would become, to many, more important than the health of the world. They planned and provided safeguards on Earth itself. But they could not see into the murkier parts of the Otherworld. They assumed that the sanctity of death was unbreakable, but they were wrong."

"Remember when I said, the afterlife is a place for peace, rest and reflection? There is no ego, selfishness, need for recognition. Existence there is different, with no industry, no money, no need for food or drink – just the potential for peace, calm and reflection. When I returned to Sherwood Forest to become its guardian, I often thought back to my time in the Otherworld; remembering was like meditation. While Sherwood Forest is itself a place full of goodness, it is a living place on Earth which is different from the tranquillity found in the land of the dead. I eventually created one place where I could mimic my time in the astral plane, where I could occasionally step away from the burden of being a protector. Look."

The ghost pointed to the other side of the clearing – to the Major Oak. "Can you see that big branch, maybe twenty feet up, that has the bright green bed of leaves? If I climbed up there first thing in the morning and sat with my back against the trunk, legs stretched out, if I took deep breaths and felt the breeze on my cheeks and arms, the warmth of the tree through my back, closed my eyes and listened to the birds and the creatures below foraging, that – for me – was as close as I could get to the Otherworld. No one in the afterlife cared who I was; in my time there, I am sure I passed by your ancestors from Africa, Mabel, yours from India, Emma and many Yorkshire folk too. We were all the same – just looking for and growing into peace."

There was a sense of that peace that settled now over the gathered team as they stared at the Major Oak and heard the same sounds that Robin Hood had described in the forest. And then their leader began to speak again. "But mankind is mankind, and, for some, peace is not worth seeking. It was Merlin; there is that name again. Merlin has his hand in everything. I heard Merlin's whispered voice eventually, one day or night, in the Otherworld and it beckoned me as if in a dream to a tree I had not seen before. The whisper told me it was the axis mundi and if I climbed it with him – with Merlin – we would find ourselves in Sherwood Forest again; and we did. We emerged, like smoke, in a glade of oaks. And that is how I became a guardian, at Merlin's urging. And that is where he comes at sunrise on the first day of each month. We talk like friends and he guides me forward.

"Merlin eventually told me about darker magic forming in a corner of the Otherworld – a magic that called to the dead who eschewed peace. There were no individuals to point to – just the same men and women who had craved personal profit and success throughout time: lords, barons, slave owners, landowners, industrialists, financiers; and joining them were sorcerers and witches stirring cauldrons of hate. That is who we face on this quest. The Mau Forest in Kenya was apparently surrounded by dark ghosts and a recruited army of living criminals who overwhelmed it. The same happened to the Amazon. The leaders of the ghouls, Merlin says, are not the spirits of individuals, but a toxic brew of evil. He calls them the Goblins of Greed."

As Robin Hood finished talking, it was clear that a sense of doom had settled over the team. The idea of the quest had been daunting enough but the description of their opponents made it sound like they were stepping into a horror movie.

"Try to relax, my friends. Apprehension is natural when you come close to a battle." Hua Mulan levelled a disarming and calming smile at the group. "We want to send you off on your mission as part of a team. If we truly join forces, our friendship can defeat any kind of cold, hateful force. Our plan is that the relationships you have formed as child and ghost will become stronger on this mission. You will have a partner, a companion, a guardian angel. You see, as a spirit, I can join you, be inside your body without being seen and can be helpful. This is what we want to do when we leave for the Białowieża Forest."

"Isn't that called possession?" asked Richard.

"If the spirit that enters your body wants to take control of you—yes, but we do not want to control, we want to help. Having said that, if we face true danger, there are ways that a ghost can exert more influence to aid you. But we would only do that with your permission, and we would never be in complete control."

Emma looked at her brother and then at each of the friends in turn. She was a little hesitant at having a ghost enter her body but then again, they had come this far, and it would be good to have help. Also, it wasn't like it would be just any ghost. "Let's do this!" she said confidently.

Robin Hood and his fellow ghosts prepared themselves. "Each of us know our companions and I do not see any reason why we should wait to test this. My friends, please stand and prepare yourselves for an experience which will be new to you all."

The protectors got to their feet and all looked anxious, some more than others, but none were scared. They had become used to surprises by now and they stood in Loxley Chase which, as Billy had said, managed to soak up fear and replace it with calmness.

Calmness also radiated from the spirits who now stood opposite them; and as the friends once again looked at some of the most impactful figures in history, all concern was wiped away to be replaced by excitement and anticipation. Emma was first and ran her hands through her hair as Hua Mulan walked forward. The ghost stood nose to nose with her partner, took one more step and then disappeared. To all in the clearing, Emma looked the same. There was no change except for the disappearance of the warrior, but for Emma herself, it was as if she had stepped under a hot shower as her skin tingled and her mind and body flooded with warmth. It was not an unpleasant feeling and after a few seconds, the sensations passed until the only change for her was the sense that there was someone behind her. She turned and looked over her shoulder but there was no one there so she took a deep breath and tried to relax.

Next, King Arthur moved forward and walked towards and into James, causing him to breathe in deeply. It was an immense presence to absorb – a true legend – but as with Emma, after the initial shock, just the feeling of companionship remained. Ada Lovelace followed suit, becoming one with Leah; Hippocrates stepped into Richard, Gouyen into Mabel and finally Hongi Hika into Billy.

Eventually, the clearing held six children standing and facing Robin Hood, but they were without doubt six children who were different, different than just moments before, different than ever before.

Robin moved away, drew his sword and shouted a challenge at James, who, in turn, pulled his bang staff from his back. At first, their parries and thrusts were normal and like in practice, James matched them. But this was no longer just practice, and Robin Hood began to use his extra strength and skill, threatening to overpower the boy. Just when it seemed like he would have to surrender, James felt a surge of energy in his arms and chest and he began to move forward, his own blows and attacks matching the archer's, meaning the swordsmanship on display was dazzling to those who were watching. As Emma looked on, at first afraid for her brother and then amazed at the skill he began to show, she found herself studying the moves of the two men. Gradually, she began to admire but also critique in her mind, thinking that she might have used an overhead cut here, or a side cut there, a parry riposte instead of just a parry. After a few minutes, she gasped in surprise, then understood that she had gained a tactical knowledge of fighting that she had never had before, or more to the point, her new companion Hua Mulan was passing on knowledge, sharing her skills.

Eventually, the swordfight came to an end but not before Robin had poked out his sword to inflict a small cut on James' arm.

Quickly, he called to Richard. "Show me which plant might heal the boy's wound." Richard looked bewildered at first but ran to the edge of the clearing and stared around at the shrubs and bushes that grew beneath the trees. To start with, he saw nothing that might help, but then the leaves and plants began to seem recognisable and before long, one patch of vegetation drew him in like a magnet. He plucked off a leaf and ran to James, placing it flat on his arm, directly over the cut.

"Good. That is the yarrow plant which is very potent. It stops bleeding and helps with healing." Robin Hood gave Richard a pat on the shoulder then stood aside as

Mabel and Billy walked to the centre of the clearing. Both unsheathed their bang staffs and then began an intricate, ceremonial dance, using the weapon as an accessory in their movements. It could not have been a dance that they both knew; there had been no time to practice. But, still, they moved in unison. Their choreography took them forward and back, side to side, stretching arms high and low. Then, suddenly, Mabel reached out with her free hand, pointing to the Major Oak, uttered a one-word command in what must have been the Apache language and a small stone flew from the base of the tree and stopped, hovering just in front of her face. Billy then barked another command from Hongi Hika and the stone shot far across the clearing and out onto the trail, flying straight into the tree that they had used for archery target practice.

Mabel and Billy both turned to the group, bowed and then Mabel said, "We are in Sherwood Forest so the magic is strong. But, remember, you carry magic with you in your weapon, which was made from the Major Oak. When you fight, in other realms, use it."

Mabel smiled, excited to be relaying important information to her team, straight from the mind of Gouyen. She then high-fived Billy and they moved to the edge of the clearing to watch.

Last to try out her partnership was Leah and she kept her demonstration simple. "In around the twelfth century, Sherwood Forest covered 100,000 acres of land. It now covers ten. When Robin Hood was alive, there were over 1000 ancient trees like the Major Oak in the forest. Now, it is the last of its kind. Together, we will undo this wrong, in

Sherwood and in other great woodlands around the world."

Robin Hood signalled to everyone to return to their logs. As they sat once more, the ghosts reappeared and came to stand beside their leader. "How did that feel for you all? Do you think having a companion will help with your quest, or hinder it?"

There were smiles all around and the friends began to chatter at once, describing the added senses or skills they had felt inside their bodies and minds when the ghosts had moved forward to help. "I say bring it on, bring those tyrants, demons, ghouls, whatever they are, bring it on." Billy was on his feet, still pumped full of the energy that came with having Hongi Hika inside his body.

"That's good, good that you have positive feelings and energy now. But, as Mabel said, remember where you are. You are inside Loxley Chase, on home soil, protected by Mother Nature herself. Soon, you will be over the channel and moving through terrain where enemy forces hide and plot." Robin pulled a map out of his tunic and spread it out on the floor. All the friends and ghosts gathered around as Robin traced a route that took them over the sea, through France, Belgium, Germany, Poland and eventually into Belarus. It was staggering to see on paper where they were going, staggering for a group of teenagers who had never set foot outside of their own country before. Now, they were going to travel through four countries to battle evil, find the grail and save the world.

"I would say it is a coincidence, but I wonder if there are coincidences any more or just magic at work. We are going straight through the region where I was born, where I was adopted." James said the words solemnly. Emma put her arm around her brother and all the friends and ghosts smiled and nodded their heads at this revelation. No—they did not think it was a coincidence.

Robin Hood spoke again quietly. "We leave on the first day of the New Year and we hope to be gone for two weeks. I will travel with you in a solid form and we will play the role of a teacher and his group of students. Our plan is to use public transport—buses and trains as much as possible because we believe we eventually will be followed and want to be on the lookout for pursuit, want to begin to understand our enemy as soon as possible. The plan is to go straight to the Białowieża Forest, find the grail and then come straight back to Loxley. Of course, that is the plan, but plans go awry."

Leah looked up from the map. "How can we be gone for two weeks without anyone noticing?"

The archer looked at each friend individually. "More magic. Mother Earth is on our side." Raising one hand, Robin Hood pointed at James' chest and then curled his fingers backwards, beckoning something on. The boy felt a sensation not unlike the one he had had when King Arthur entered him, only this time a spectral figure of himself walked out of his body and stood next to Robin Hood. "It does you no harm to leave your shadow behind, and, in the same way you have a companion, we will assign an ally ghost from the Otherworld to step into and guide your image. No one will notice. Each of your alter egos will be bewitched and will be you for twenty-one days at the most before its strength will fail. And if we are gone for more than twenty-one days, alas, I think our own strength will have failed."

The Quest
One

Christmas was strange for Emma and James. Their father had been allowed to leave hospital because it was the holiday and he had shown some remarkable improvement. Robin Hood had let them keep the staff in his room for over a week, because Excalibur was active and had more than enough power when in the hands of King Arthur to keep Sherwood Forest healthy. Specialists had come and gone to study the miracle that was Mr Trueman, but none of them had paid attention to the old stick leaning up against his bed.

But the stick was leaving soon, would be needed in Białowieża Forest. The brother and sister knew they needed to bring the grail back with them from their adventure, for the good of planet Earth, but also for their dad.

They received some nice presents, had too much to eat as usual and played board games with their mother and father, as their parents insisted they do every year. Outside of the living room window, they could see snow falling; and in the back of their minds, they wondered about Loxley Chase and how it would look under a blanket of white. The rest of their friends could not get away because of family celebrations, but the two of them went to visit the wood once, on Boxing Day. They made the excuse that they needed some exercise to help digest the mounds of turkey and mince pies they had eaten, but instead spent all of their time with Robin Hood, just sitting and listening to stories from the past, stories of how life had been for the outlaws in Sherwood Forest, the real tactics they had used to avoid the Sheriff of Nottingham and how their love for the true king and for England kept them going through many hardships.

It was cold in the clearing but huddled around a blazing fire with the legend himself telling tales that described his band of 'Merry Men' – Little John, Friar Tuck, Will Scarlet, Much the Miller's Son and Alan-a-Dale – it did not feel cold. In fact, there was enough warmth and cheer to keep them in Loxley Chase way past the time they said they would return home. They made Robin Hood talk in detail about how exactly Prince John and the Sheriff of Nottingham had taken the throne while Richard the Lionheart was away fighting in France; and what had made Robin Hood decide it was possible to provide a haven for the poor who were threatened and bullied, deep in the forest. They wanted to know what it was like, waiting and fighting until the rightful king could return. Listening to these tales caused many magical hours to pass by in a flash and the thought that they would soon be travelling with this man, this hero, to create their own adventure, their own legend, was more exciting than they could bear. The New Year could not come soon enough.

And, of course, it arrived in a flash. New Year's Day was a Sunday, not an involved family holiday, so it was easy for all to get away and meet as a group in Loxley Chase. The morning was chilly with a frost on the ground and a breeze blowing that numbed exposed noses and ears, until that is they made it up the hill and into the wood where the shelter of the trees calmed the air. Festive robins hopped about in branches above and red squirrels and a pair of foxes scuttled along the path as they walked, until they met the big bear from the spirit world ambling ahead of them. That sight made the living creatures scatter into the trees.

In the clearing, all the ghosts were waiting, and, even though they were great figures that had lived through some of the most monumental times in history, there seemed to be a level of excitement on each of their faces. Emma saw the emotion and tried to imagine what it was like to have lived a life of importance and then be given a chance to sample that level of excitement again. Here were ghosts from many different geographical locations and periods of time, suddenly united with a chance to save the world. What an adventure this would be, even for them.

Robin Hood was all business. He was honest enough to ask them one more time if they were ready and willing to go through with the plan and each of the friends nodded, eager and anxious at the same time. Then he had them line up and quickly and quietly he pointed at each individual and beckoned shadows forward so that they stood, shimmering noiselessly across from their bodies. Next, a group of six ghosts of men and women, long dead but summoned to help from the Otherworld, appeared out of the trees and moved into the spirits of the children, instantly solidifying them so that they looked real and whole.

"They will suffice. They have your voices and

mannerisms and memories so they will suffice for three weeks. They will not be exact, of course, but each of the ghosts will play their roles with slight head colds, slight fevers so the strangeness will be passed off as illness. It should work, but what do you think?" the archer asked.

The protectors looked at their shadow-doubles and were amazed to be looking at themselves. Richard stepped forward and prodded himself, but there was no response. Leah looked at herself and asked the question, "Who are you?"

The spirit responded immediately, "I am Leah."

Intrigued, James also spoke to his double. "Which is the best football team in the country?"

His spirit also answered immediately, "Leeds United, of course. What are you, stupid?"

All the ghosts and children present laughed long and hard at that response and all present agreed that the spirits would do, that they may well be able to pull off this trick. The laughter died down eventually and without any goodbyes or thanks, the fake children were waved off down the pathway so that they could make their way to their homes to finish off New Year's Day with unsuspecting families. The protectors themselves were now anxious to set off, tired of imagining what this journey would be like and eager to just live it. Recognizing this, the ghosts each moved towards, then stepped into their companion; and, without another word, the group set off down the pathway. When free from the trees, they turned left and headed off, slightly away from the village towards an outlying bus stop.

Emma commented on Robin Hood's general look, as

he led the way – a solid, colourful version of himself with regular clothes. "It's just a strategy," he told her. "A way for us to look somewhat normal as a group, but also for us to not reveal our full force until we have to." She was just pleased to have her friends around her and her companion in place, and content that the quest had begun and her brother was happy. His own personal mission to save their father was in full flow now.

Two

The travel across Britain was exhilarating and eye-opening for all. It was like a fun field trip but with an added level of secrecy that made it even more exciting. Each of the group members had started the journey bundled up against the cold with scarves wrapped around their necks, various hats on heads and deep pocketed coats pulled tight around bodies. This lasted until they crossed the Loxley village border and then, suddenly, the air temperature went way up and they had to peel every layer off but one.

"Is that our first experience with climate change? And the protection Sherwood Forest gives Loxley?" Leah's question was met with grim-faced looks and nods from the ghosts.

They stowed their extra clothes away in a locker at the station and then could have been any group of travelling family or friends, sitting on a bus to London and a train to the East Coast, down into the channel tunnel across to France. Except they weren't just anyone, they were runaways with spiritual stand-ins fooling their parents, runaways led by the ghost of Robin Hood. How hilarious was that! So hilarious that the children regularly huddled together to whisper and laugh out loud, then they could hardly keep straight faces as they went through security in France, showed their IDs, wondering what on earth had been on Robin Hood's ID! There were no issues, however;

no awkward questions about an adult travelling with six children in tow and they made it onto European mainland soil without incident.

The atmosphere of the trip changed as soon as they settled onto a train that would take them across France and Belgium to Berlin in Germany. They had a carriage to themselves with a constant air conditioning hum so they could talk freely. Robin Hood sat next to the window, looking out, and said immediately, "I wasn't completely sure of myself when I said that Loxley Chase was the last wood in the country, but I didn't see even one tree as we travelled. Did you? And England used to be a country of waterways but all I saw were dry riverbeds. It looks like the Earth is in a worse position than even I thought."

It was strange and a little unsettling to see a disappointed ghost, especially when that ghost was the strong and certain Robin Hood. Emma wondered when was the last time he had travelled outside of Loxley. Thinking back, when they had left the village, the snow had stopped immediately and they had journeyed through town after town and city after city on their way to the coast of Britain, with very few breaks in buildings that she could remember. Now, she also looked out of the window as they sped through France and saw the same thing, lines of houses, office buildings and smokestacks whizzing by as the train sped further east along its tracks. Grey was definitely the colour of the world outside Loxley Chase.

Their leader recovered his composure quickly and pulled out a map to show them again the route they were taking. There was total concentration now from the team as they looked down and saw a red line that went from

Calais to Brussels, from Brussels to Berlin and then from Berlin to their destination, Brest. The attentiveness was mixed with real nervousness as reality again hit home; they were in the middle of an adventure. They were travelling many miles from Loxley in a strange land and had no idea what might happen once they reached their destination deep in Eastern Europe.

As if Robin Hood had read their minds, he spoke to them in more positive tones. "You need to start to be aware of what we are doing from this moment on. We have left Britain and I have no doubt that spies from our enemies will be looking for us. We need to start being alert and self-assured. We need to ready ourselves for action at any minute. I have asked your partners to begin to help you be more confident. You are young and innocent and, therefore, are the perfect people for this quest, but you are also inexperienced whereas your companions have lots of experience. I've asked them to share their accomplishments and the feelings that come with success as we travel."

As each of the ghosts, still hidden inside the bodies of the children, began to talk about some of their greatest moments, the great victories, successes and challenges from their living years, the train carriage that they were in seemed to hum with energy.

Emma and James could feel the energy, could feel that this was an important moment on their quest. They could feel it personally as their own bodies and minds filled with the passion of achievement and greatness, but they could also feel it and see it in their friends, in the closed eyes and faraway smiles. This was the moment when the ghosts really joined forces with them, became true companions as they travelled towards fear and danger.

After sufficient time had passed for them to listen and converse, Robin asked everyone to share what they had learned. He wanted the entire group to have a deeper understanding of all their colleagues – those who would be alongside them, helping them overcome obstacles as they got closer to their goal. Emma deliberately kept quiet and it was Richard who spoke first, his eyes still full of amazement as he described the feeling of knowing how beneficial medicine could be to mankind – that it was not magic but science that led to true mastery of the healing art. Then he told of one of Hippocrates' most testing achievements, successfully completing an operation on a man's chest in 400 BC. This was thousands of years before modern medical instruments and X-rays, when physicians would prescribe healing balms and tonics for everything, and not use surgery. To have a man's life, literally in your hands, using an innovative form of treatment with no support structure in place was truly astounding.

Leah went next and explained how Ada Lovelace had been the daughter of one of the greatest English poets of all time, Lord Byron, but had still found her own path in science. Her biggest challenge had been keeping her nerve when she had to read aloud her famous notes, the notes that were now considered a pathway to modern computer programming, explaining them to a room full of prejudiced men who believed science was not for women.

James focused on the most memorable of so many battles in King Arthur's career when on Mount Badon, he had finally defeated the Saxon invaders who had been attacking Britain for many years; and he had defeated them with one of the greatest cavalry charges in history. So powerful was James' description, the group could almost hear the huge white horses, hooves pounding and breath snorting as they routed the enemy shield walls. For a few minutes, imaginations were louder than the sound of the train as it clattered along the track, over the Belgian border, deeper and deeper into Europe.

When he was done, James looked around the carriage and understood again why Robin Hood was such a good leader. Not only were a group of teenagers more appreciative of the trials great historical figures had been through in the past, but the great historical figures themselves, many of them from times that were centuries apart, also began to value what their peers had been through, years before they were born or years after they were dead.

Robin Hood stood and took down a basket of food that he had bought in Calais and started to pass out sandwiches and drinks to the protectors. "This is, indeed, a gathering of greats. I am proud to be a part of this team, a team that is full of individuals that have accomplished so much. Three more to go, so, Mabel, let us hear from you."

Mabel teared up as she began to talk about her partner. "There are several incidents I could talk about to let you know how brave and daring a wife, mother and tribal leader my partner was. But, sadly, the greatest achievement for Gouyen was maintaining her pride and dignity when she was jailed by the American army as a prisoner of war, a war which had been a fight for the survival of the Apache nation facing eradication from their native lands."

Ghosts and protectors alike joined Mabel in a moment of silence after her story, and then all eyes fell on Billy. "Hongi Hika and I agree that the best stories he can tell and the best lessons we can learn from him involve negotiation and cooperation. He talked to me about being afraid – for himself and his people – when physically fighting in battle, but being more afraid, facing greater obstacles, when he tried to convince his own leaders and followers that compromise was possible. He is not sure if there is any room for diplomacy in the war we fight, but he urges us to mix compassion with our ferocity."

Finally, it was time for Emma. She had waited until last, following the advice of Hua Mulan. "The general has spent much of our story time just looking at her companions, admiring her companions and listening to all the great tales from the past. She is humbled to be surrounded by such leaders, leaders in battle and in society, leaders in science and the science of care and health. She considers her greatest triumphs to have come while serving her people but thinks an even bigger triumph may be on the horizon, as she walks into battle shoulder to shoulder with new and great friends."

It had been a small speech, but that made it nonetheless impressive. All were moved by the words of a very brave woman, including Emma herself, and again the mood in the carriage hinted at a growing confidence – a growing togetherness that was a good sign for the quest. They sat quietly for a while, eating and drinking and looking out of the window at the crowded expanse of Belgium. The buildings and streets were like those in

Britain, perhaps a little more modern with wider highways, but similar. There were lots of people driving and walking in all directions, rushing from one place to another, minds focused on work or personal lives, inward-looking with no time to open their eyes and wonder at the drab lifelessness of their surroundings. Most of those on foot or riding bikes were wearing face masks, wary of the unclean air.

"So can we talk a little more about what's going to happen, what our plan is?" James asked the question, rubbing his hands together as though he was itching to do something.

"Of course," said their leader, and he pointed to the map which was still laid out on the floor of the carriage. "We are going to change trains in Brussels even though this one continues to our destination. We can eat there and keep our eyes open for any individuals or groups that are tailing us, then catch a later train and move on to Berlin where we will stop again to get some sleep. The next day, we will move on to Brest. If we have time and if our followers – our enemies – allow us time, we will find a hotel which will be our base. We will then scout the city and will eventually head there where we think we will find the grail." Robin had pointed at a green patch on the map, just to the south of Brest, a large expanse of woodland – the Białowieża Forest. "If we do not have time, are pursued or are in danger, we will make straight for a safe house at the edge of the trees."

"On the map, it looks like a nice, big forest. Is it like Loxley Chase?" Mabel asked the question, prompted by Gouyen who, because she had been a refugee for much of her life, was always interested in the details of a new destination.

"My understanding is that the forest itself is like Loxley Chase, but the surrounding area is not. Britain has some advantages being an island, in how climate change has impacted it and in how Sherwood Forest and the power of nature can protect it. Here, the forest is in the middle of a dark industrial land full of anger and sadness. The Brest region, the border area between Belarus and Poland as a whole, has become lawless – a place for criminals and thugs. Regular people do not venture near to the Białowieża Forest and those that do pay a price."

"And we still do not know who might be following us and who might be waiting for us?" Emma kept the stream of questions coming. All the group were now leaning forward in their seats, staring down at the map. Everyone sensed that the ghosts within them knew details about this quest but were keeping quiet because it was important that their young partners ask questions and learn. They also sensed the ghosts leaning in themselves, as though they were looking over each living person's shoulder to listen, to see if there were any new facts that might come to light. It was the strangest sensation, and it was tempting again to turn and look, though, of course, there would be nothing to see.

"We are not sure, I'm afraid, Emma. There are sure to be ghosts there like us, but to what extent they are helping people like we are helping you, that is unclear. As we have mentioned, we know some of the details of what happened in Kenya and Brazil – that there was a large force, a mix of ghosts and recruited thugs, and the destruction was devastating."

A sombre mood settled over the group and Robin Hood was quiet for a few minutes, waiting to see if there were any more questions. When he heard none, he folded up the map and sat back in his seat. It was getting cloudy and grim outside and lights came on in the cabin just as a loud whistle blew which told them they were approaching the station at Brussels. Silence allowed for thought, the digestion of facts about the plan of action and for the children, the constant juggling of excitement, hope and fear. The team wanted to be on this adventure, but they also wanted it to be over. They wanted to be victorious, returning with the grail in hand on this same track with the same soothing sounds of an engine chugging, wheels turning, only heading for Britain instead of an unknown place called Belarus.

The First Fight
One

It was late in the day but still warm outside as they stepped off their train onto the Belgian station. Each of the children looked around with uncertainty, unused to humidity in the winter and the look and feel of a foreign land. They walked slowly towards a small café that was in the middle of the platform, when Mabel received a gentle nudge in her mind from an ever-alert Gouyen. She marched a little quicker than normal to catch up to Robin Hood and whispered without turning her head, whispered that they were being followed. Robin linked his arm with hers to indicate that he had heard and they carried on moving forward briskly until everyone had passed through the door of the café into steamy air that smelled of sausages and coffee. The café was busy, but there was a table that they could all fit around. The children sat listening to strange languages that were being spoken and also sung softly on the radio in the background.

Robin Hood had placed himself next to Mabel and was looking down at a menu in a relaxed manner. He quietly asked the girl to nudge him under the table when the spy entered through the door. A server came around who spoke good English. She brought them all tea; and they began ordering food, but, before the waitress had even made it to the second member of the group, Robin Hood felt his ankle being kicked. He glanced up at a television screen that was showing a Brussels' football team game and out of the corner of his eye saw a big, solid man with a severely scarred face walk in wearing a leather jacket with the collar turned up. The man had strange, dark deep eyes that made it look like he hadn't slept in weeks. He walked up to the counter, sat at a stool and could clearly be seen looking at them every few minutes through a mirror that hung on the wall behind the café staff.

It was loud in the small area where they sat, so Robin Hood was not worried about being overheard and he carefully let the group know what was going on. "So here is our first real test on this mission. Mabel and Gouyen have spotted that we are being followed. Don't all look when I tell you where he is. Instead, each of you will glance that way in turn, and, when you have seen the man, you will take a drink of your tea and the next person can go. Remember, your glances need to be gentle and subtle. Leah will go first, followed by Richard, then Billy, then James and then Emma. It's the man with the black jacket sitting at the counter. Notice the slight rippling around the edges of his body. This is a ghost, not a living recruit."

It might have been amusing for each of the protectors to watch their friends' attempts at being secretive if the situation had not been so serious. Mabel's head went around in a circle, looking at everything but the man, before she stole a quick look and then picked up her cup. Billy began to whistle as he stared up at the ceiling, which caused Leah to start giggling, before he finally glanced left quickly and took a loud slurp of tea. Richard was good, looking at the TV in the same way Robin had done and catching the spy out of the corner of his eye. Emma was also subtle as she waved at the waitress who was standing at the counter, asking her for more tea and spotting the man as she did so. James was the problem. For some reason, the idea that they were being spied on had caused his temper to begin clouding his thoughts. He had a father at home who was dying, humanity was systematically destroying its own planet and some goons thought it was important to try and stop them from helping.

He stared straight at the enemy's face in the mirror, only realising he was doing so when the man began to stare back. Maybe it didn't help that his companion was one of the greatest warriors in British history, a ghost who was feeding off James' fury and was looking for any reason to fight. In fact, it definitely didn't help because it was King Arthur's urging that made James stand ready to do battle with this enemy soldier. When James stood, the man spun around in his seat and began moving towards the boy. Then, six of his big, dark-eyed friends burst through the door and the protectors were involved in their first real action.

It may not have been a good thing tactically, to expose themselves so early in the search for the grail, but it did feel like a good thing practically for the friends, because now they could begin to understand exactly how fighting might work on this mission. Their only real combat skills had been against ghosts who were their colleagues. What needed to happen against bad guys? And when they had practiced, they had been fighting alone. How would this work with a ghost inside – coordinated action moves?

Many questions were answered early as each

individual stood, partly because they saw a friend being threatened and partly because their companions had urged them up. As each of the attackers came at them with their own weapons – knives, clubs, crowbars, sticks – so each of the team found themselves reaching backwards, drawing out their bang staffs, anxious to put them to use, holding them tight. They were ready to do battle, nervous with dry mouths and clammy hands; and then a twang echoed from behind them and they saw a spy explode in a cloud of smoke.

A burning smell filled the air as Robin's arrow made the lead attacker at the door disappear in a puff of smoke and then chaos ensued. James parried a swinging lead pipe, Mabel charged forward screaming and whirling her bang staff around her head and there were shrieks and yells from the people sitting and standing in the café. They had been trained well in Loxley Chase, that much was clear, because most of the protectors immediately began to fight with the enemy one on one and each of them seemed to overpower their opponent quickly. James parried again and thrust and his attacker went pop, while Emma parried twice and then slashed down at her opponent's head and poof. Mabel did not even need to parry because her howling assault seemed to freeze her target and her stick came slashing around from the left and her enemy exploded with a louder bang than most. Richard and Leah had stayed back and were analysing the battle, looking for clues and occurrences that might help them later, but Billy was in a prolonged duel. He parried well and tried to attack but his opponent seemed quicker than most, or he was slower. He parried two more times in succession a little frantically and then there was whisper in his mind and he pretended to jab, causing the enemy to try to block, then kicked the man between the legs and stabbed him, causing a cloud of blue smoke to appear.

Their first fight was over and each of the friends looked around the café, stunned that it had happened. Robin Hood did not allow them to relax, however; he was anxious to leave before there was trouble from the customers who looked panicked and frightened, or from the police who were bound to have been called. Robin ushered them quickly out of the door and pointed at a train across from the one they'd arrived in – a big locomotive with a long line of carriages that had slowly begun to inch forward. They sprinted away from the café, Billy reaching the end wagon first and holding a door open for the rest who jumped on just as the train began to gather speed. Luckily, there were two empty carriages at the back of what seemed like a quiet commuter train, and so they hastily found seats and slumped down, catching their breaths. Their hearts and minds were still racing from the fight and James had a smile on his face as he leaned his head back on the cushioned chair.

Two

"I think a team meeting would be good – with all members present, please." Robin Hood had a stern look on his face and was standing with his back to the compartment door, facing them all. Each of the friends felt a slight tug as the ghosts left their bodies and came forward to sit or stand around the cabin. Ada Lovelace positioned herself next to Robin as a lookout, but all seemed quiet still as the train gathered more pace and began speeding through Belgian cities and towns.

"I will get to the point quickly. James, if your personal feelings are more important than this quest then I need you to leave now. Our king will accompany you back to Britain and we will continue on our own."

James looked devastated and a tear appeared in the corner of his eye, while King Arthur looked dangerously upset. "Please be careful with what you say next, Robin Hood. I have been the companion of James Trueman for only a few days, but he has become my friend. If you dishonour him, you dishonour me."

Each of the young protectors was now experiencing a complex mix of emotions. The effects of the fight were catching up with them, and they began to understand one of the key benefits of having the ghosts present in their bodies. The fear and anxiety that had been mostly squashed earlier now appeared, washing away feelings of strength and confidence. Also, if fighting for their lives had been hard enough, now two legendary figures from the past were arguing and it looked like their band of brothers and sisters was about to break up before they had even made it to their destination.

"Of course, I will be careful with the words I use, my king. In fact, I will show you honour immediately by offering you the leadership of this group. You are a great man and a great king. There is nothing I could do that you couldn't; in fact, perhaps you would be better in my place." Robin Hood bowed his head slightly as he finished and the look on King Arthur's face changed from one of anger to one of peace.

"I do not want to replace you, Robin. You know that. Speak and I will listen and follow."

Robin Hood nodded and then turned to James. "I consider you a friend now, too, James Trueman, but I lead a team and must consider the team. I understand your anger, but we have something we need to achieve; and if we are to be successful, you must listen and follow. Do you understand?"

Tears were flowing freely down James' cheeks now and he nodded his head, a look of shame on his face. Emma put her arm around her brother's shoulder and then King Arthur himself stepped forward and knelt in front of the boy. James looked up, still crying, but the look of shame was replaced with one of awe as the great king took his hand.

"James, the mistake here is more mine than yours. I am an experienced warrior and I should have shown restraint, but I have to say, it was a pleasure fighting with you." The king squeezed the boy's hand, stood and returned to his corner, leaving James with a tear-stained but happier expression.

Robin Hood's face relaxed. "Thank you, my king. Yes, you all fought well and I am proud, but we need to be prepared for tougher battles ahead."

Hua Mulan was nodding her head vigorously and turned to address the group. "Remember, it takes many battles to win a war and this was just one battle. I think it was clear that we were just challenged by foot soldiers – the weakest members of our enemy's forces. They were low-level ghosts sent to find out our location and our strengths and weaknesses. Unfortunately, they know where we are, but the better news is that we showed we are strong. This was good practice for you, my young friends. Yes, you did well, but we must drill some more because I fear the soldiers we meet next will be stronger, tougher and full of evil."

And practice they did. They left their compartment, checked to make sure their carriage was still empty and then put Hippocrates at one end to keep guard. The corridor that ran the length of the carriage was not wide, but the back section – reserved for luggage and bikes – was an open space and so allowed for the swinging and thrusting of weapons, making it a perfect training area.

There were little things in the fight that King Arthur and Hua Mulan – the close combat experts – had noticed and wanted to correct, and so one of these specialists would actively practice and one would watch. They focused on footwork and balance and especially on the way that ghost and person could act together – a new and beneficial option for the protectors, one they had not had time to work on back in Loxley. After a few hours, it became easier to adjust quickly based on the thoughts and instincts of the ghosts and both instructors commented on this improvement as they fought.

"Why do you not just take us over completely? Would we not be even better then?" Emma wanted to try and understand everything, before they made it to Belarus, so that she would be prepared for whatever happened.

"No, because they are your bodies and minds, not ours. Enhancing your thoughts and reflexes is good, but taking over you would involve removing your own instincts and skills. That would be bad. No. If we succeed, we succeed together." Robin Hood seemed to like the fact that they were asking questions and he was patient with his answers.

"What if you left us and fought on your own? There would be more of us and it would be easier to win, wouldn't it?" Richard scratched his chin as he posed a question.

"Again, I think we are stronger together. The enemies you just fought against were ghosts and technically we could have beaten them, but together we beat them easily. We will come up against actual people – very soon, I am sure – and then we will really need teamwork. No, let us try to always stick together. We have more chance of victory."

The best practice fight of all now involved James with King Arthur inside him against Emma and Hua Mulan. James was strong anyway, but when, perhaps, the greatest warrior Britain had ever seen was working with him, he became formidable. The recent fight had allowed Emma to begin to feel in tune with her ghost; and Hua Mulan was a ferocious fighter, especially when she was helping and protecting a friend. When they practiced against each other, everyone turned to look and admire as jabs and thrusts were blocked and hard swings parried, causing thuds and loud bangs to echo around the carriage.

When they were all back in their compartment resting and eating, Emma asked one more question. "Why is it that you are solid and strong when the other ghosts are not?" She was looking at Robin Hood as she spoke. All her friends looked up to listen to the answer. This was something they had all been intrigued about.

"It is Sherwood Forest. I became its guardian and because of that role, I gained magical benefits and strengths that other ghosts do not have. I am constantly surrounded by trees and animals and there is potency in that. As you know, you, yourselves, are drawing on that energy too. And we will need every advantage we can find. We will face a darker magic sooner or later. I mentioned evil has grown as a presence in the astral plane and sorcery will be used. We should be ready."

The whistle on the train blew again which told them they were in Germany and about to pull into the Berlin station. The ghosts moved back into the bodies of their friends; and even though the presence of a companion brought renewed energy, still the children were very tired. It was now late in the evening and they had been travelling for nearly two days, sleeping only on the train from England to France. They each needed a bed and several hours of rest, but as they made to leave their carriage, they heard noises on the station and realised sleep was a long way off. Robin Hood leaned out of the carriage window and saw a line of police with dogs ahead talking to and searching every passenger that left the train. Obviously, their battle in the café had attracted attention. Armed men were also walking towards the train and there would only be a few moments before they were discovered.

Pulling his head back inside, Robin gave instructions. "Okay, do you remember the important ethical rule I have alluded to a few times? The one where possession is bad? Well, we're going to break that rule now." Everyone looked confused so he told them what was going on outside the train. "Please trust us and we'll show you another benefit of working closely with ghosts."

The children nodded, and then each of them experienced the ghost over their shoulders moving forward and becoming them, until they all felt like they were now behind themselves, looking over their own shoulders. It was as if they had swapped places with the ghosts; and, at first, it gave each of them a panicky feeling – a feeling that they had lost control of their own minds and bodies. But then soothing sensations appeared, emanating from their companions. They realised that the ghosts were friends, that they meant no harm, that they would be themselves and control themselves as soon as the danger had passed.

Everyone stood still; and they saw several police officers get onto the train and begin to walk down the corridor, looking into each of the doors – obviously searching for people. Since they were at the end of the train, their door was one of the first opened and all of the inhabitants held their breaths, waiting to be discovered, but then it was closed again and the policemen moved on down the train.

"What happened?" whispered James, except he realised quickly that the whisper was only in his own head because he no longer had control of his mouth.

"We're invisible. When we are in control of a body, we can keep it solid or make it ghost-like. Other ghosts can see us, but, to people, we are invisible," King Arthur whispered aloud, answering James' question but also making sure the rest of the group knew what was happening.

Once the police searching the train had moved into the next carriage, Robin Hood led the way out of their compartment and down onto the platform. It was relatively quiet, apart from a slow stream of passengers that were heading towards the main station and the exit. There they were being stopped and questioned. There was a gap between a line of police officers and the edge of the platform where the railway tracks ended and that was where Robin led his team. He signalled to them with his hand to get into a single file because the gap was only five or six feet wide and a young policeman on the end was swinging a rifle and banging it against his foot as he waited and watched, clearly bored and unhappy to be there when he could be involved in real detective work. Robin Hood moved over to the very edge of the platform, his friends followed and they quickly walked through and past before the swinging rifle could connect with anyone and give them away.

Just as they thought they were safe, a big dog who was standing with his handler, sniffing passengers, twisted its head and started barking madly, staring in the direction of the protectors. Soldiers and police turned and looked the way the dog was facing, but when they saw nothing, they shouted at it to be quiet. It knew there was something there, though, because the smell of boys, girls and ghosts was a powerful one. It carried on barking and tugging on its leash, begging to be set free to explore. Robin did not want to take any chances and so broke into a run towards the exit gate, urging his companions to follow. As they were getting close, Hua Mulan looked back and saw the handler of the guard dog reaching down to unleash it. He trusted his canine partner and it was highly unusual for it to be barking at nothing. As soon as it was free, the big German shepherd ran at full speed, following its nose, towards the line of retreating suspects. All of them were hopping over a fence, but just as Richard sprang, the dog arrived and managed to grab the very bottom of his shoe. There was a brief tussle, then Richard fell over the gate and all the friends ran as quickly as they could, down the street and around a corner. The dog was left with a white Umbro running shoe in his mouth. Because it was no longer part of boy and ghost, it had ceased to be invisible. When the handler and a fellow policeman arrived, they took the sneaker from the dog and looked closely at it, puzzled. Richard was running unevenly in his one shoe, but the group still managed to keep going for several blocks before they stopped to catch their breath and plan. They seemed to have escaped but wouldn't feel safe until they were off the streets. The ghosts were in tune with the bodies they were inhabiting and it was clear that the protectors were exhausted. Hongi Hika had overseen the route and sleeping arrangements and so he guided them to the nearest hotel. They had decided to stay invisible in case the search was still on or in case a description of a man with a group of children had been circulated, but when they made it close to a towering Hilton, Robin Hood became whole and normal so that he could reserve a room. Again, winding past a small crowd and through the doors to the hotel was not an easy task for seven people when only one was visible, but they made it to the reception desk where they got a big double suite. They all trooped to the nearest elevator, made sure they were the only ones going up, exited at the tenth floor and finally walked into a safe room where ghosts moved out of children and children collapsed onto two king-size beds and two sofas.

Sleep was instantaneous for some, not so for others as adrenaline continued to flow. But they had been awake for so long that tiredness eventually dragged all the friends into unconsciousness. The ghosts, without any need for rest, were content to move into the adjoining room to talk about the day's events.

Three

When Emma and James were shaken awake, it was dark in the room and they were completely disoriented. Robin Hood stood over them with his fingers to his lips. He pointed to the rest of the protectors, still sprawled on the beds, sound asleep. They climbed up quietly and tiptoed out of the bedroom into the next suite where the ghosts were waiting anxiously.

"There is trouble outside. We have been discovered and challenged, not by the police but by one of our enemies. This enemy, I fear, is much stronger than the ghosts we met in the café." Robin was calm in describing the situation to them, but there was more than a hint of seriousness behind his voice.

Emma tried to match his calmness. "What can we do to help?"

"Well, we gave thought to leaving you asleep, but you are the leaders of this mission and deserve to be involved in all matters, despite your age. We must go out to meet this man. I will lead and we think you should follow, then keep out of sight to observe and learn. But it may be a dangerous situation and we would certainly understand if you would like to wait and hear from me when I return."

The response was instantaneous. "We should come."

All the ghosts joined them except for Hippocrates who volunteered to stay and guard the room. Only Robin Hood,

Emma and James were visible, but there were six people in the elevator as it slowly lowered itself to the ground floor. Their leader kept his finger on the 'close door' button as he looked closely at the two teenagers.

"There is something in the street out there, something that contacted me in a way that only ghosts can. The challenge was hard and hurtful, which means nothing except there is a level of confidence in this evil thing. He may just be a ghost in which case I am sure of my ability to best him. However, if there is something else to him, or with him, and the situation becomes dangerous, I must have your word that you will follow the lead of King Arthur and Hua Mulan. Do I have your word?"

Emma and James nodded; and as they did so, their companions stepped into their bodies and Hongi Hika, Ada Lovelace and Gouyen disappeared. Now three people walked out of the elevator and headed towards the exit; and as they did so, the two protectors felt a surge of battle readiness filling their hearts and minds. It was a humid night outside and the street was empty except for a lone figure in the distance to the right, leaning against a lamppost. While the rest of his team stayed out of sight on the porch of the hotel, Robin Hood walked forward and down the road to meet his challenger, head turning from side to side to make sure he was not being ambushed. From their hiding place, Emma and James watched the figure come out to the centre of the road; and as he did so, they heard a curse from behind them. James felt King Arthur noticeably flinch inside his body. Hua Mulan, it seemed, was less surprised.

The enemy that Robin Hood went to meet was a boy –

older than James – maybe sixteen or seventeen years old. He wore jeans, sneakers and a short-sleeved T-shirt with Legia Warszawa written across the chest. His hair was ruffled and blond, face thin with a disdainful but somewhat strained grin in place. As Robin came closer, the boy reached behind his shoulder and pulled out a long, military truncheon; and as he did so, his grin widened to a smile and his body rippled with hidden power.

Robin Hood was about to speak when the boy moved quickly into action. He was young, fast and clearly well-trained, wielding the stick like a bludgeon and looking for a way to power past his adversary's defences. But the legendary archer was good also; experienced and agile, he circled the boy and moved him around, keeping him as off balance as he could while he parried and blocked. There was a difference in the styles, that was immediately obvious – with Robin Hood overly defensive and the boy, if anything, reckless and indifferent to preventing attacks as he sought a speedy, violent victory.

As the fight continued, King Arthur and Hua Mulan stepped out of their friends and Gouyen, Hongi Hika and Ada Lovelace became visible. "We have to go down there – all of us." Hua Mulan looked concerned now although she still held her emotions in check better than the king. He was clearly livid and James was relieved that his companion had left him. It had been hard to experience that level of anger inside his body.

"I don't understand. Robin Hood looks as though he is a match for the boy. Why are you so concerned?" Emma switched her gaze between the battling foes on the street and her friends close by.

"The boy is possessed and by a strong ghost, it seems. He is fighting against his will. Robin cannot strike the boy because he will harm him and it looks like the ghost knows this. He is becoming more and more irresponsible, because he does not care if the boy is killed or not." King Arthur almost spat the words out in his fury. "We must go now before this fight brings attention. Our enemy wants to feel out our strengths and weaknesses as much as possible before they truly do battle with us, before they show their own strengths in Belarus, so let us get this thing done."

King Arthur did not wait for agreement or disagreement but surged out of hiding and began to run down the street, followed by his friends. Emma and James were close behind their king but Hua Mulan whispered to them both to stay at the rear. "There is danger here. Be careful."

They were just in time, it seemed, because the two combatants had come to a key moment in their fight. The boy had abandoned any pretence at control and was swinging wildly at Robin Hood who was parrying skilfully but somewhat frantically. There were many moments when he could have ended the fight with a swift thrust of his blade but he would not harm the boy; and, therefore, the battle went on. A particularly frenzied assault had brought him to his knees when a loud shout rang out. "Enough!" Arthur had reached the scene and it was clear the possessed boy was wary of this new challenger.

As the rest of the group arrived, the boy stepped back and laughed loudly; but, again, the look on his face was one of forced evil – a strained, delirious look. His body rippled once more and then a ghoul stepped out sideways to the left, followed by another to the right. Now, even Robin Hood – normally the calmest of leaders – looked furious and it was clear that all the ghosts recognised the wrong that had been done to the boy, being possessed by not one but two spirits. In control of his own body at last, the boy slumped to the ground, exhausted. King Arthur and his archer friend made to attack immediately. They were brought to a halt, however, by another strong command.

"Hold, Arthur, Robin." Hua Mulan came forward, her own rage hidden by a mask of control. At that moment, Emma and James could see clearly why she had been such a leader, a woman in a man's world but a woman who commanded respect and loyalty.

Behind her, Hongi Hika was moving also – sword raised – but an upheld hand from Robin Hood held him in place. There was time, a few moments as order was restored, for the brother and sister to look closely at the two enemies that had appeared. They were big muscular beings – one slightly larger than the other – almost inhuman, sexless but with arms, legs and a head. Their faces were what caught the attention immediately. They had maniacal, schizophrenic expressions as though six or seven beings were vying for control of the face muscles available. James grabbed his sister's hand, feeling openly terrified of these things.

"You have achieved your aim; now, go but leave the boy." Hua Mulan had a presence that allowed her to stand confidently in front of two powerful foes.

One of the goblins spoke with a deep, grating voice. "The boy goes with us, or he dies."

Hongi Hika inched forward but, again, Hua Mulan raised a hand to hold him in check. "You risk purgatory. Why? You have a goal here, ghost. What does killing a boy get you? You are both strong – yes, but we have the numbers to defeat you and to what end?"

"I risk nothing. You will not allow the boy to be harmed. We have seen what we wish to see and so we go. On your feet, Kurt."

The boy pulled himself up until he was standing, wobbling slightly – still exhausted from his ordeal – pain showing in his eyes. James thought of the strain he had felt when Arthur had been inside of him and the king had been angry. He couldn't imagine having two evil ghosts in his body at one time.

While the focus was on Kurt, the larger of the goblins took a few steps forward, sniffing the air as it went. "Ah, you have brought more young strays with you. Maybe a trade?" Its eyes went to James and Emma.

"Beast, make one more move towards my friends and I do not care how many souls you contain, I will cut you down." Hua Mulan had drawn her samurai sword with lightning speed and stood in a fighting stance, her efforts at diplomacy done. This clearly cowed the enemy and it took two steps back.

They could not prevent the two goblins and their captive from leaving, but Hongi Hika tried one more time while he had the chance. "Who do you serve? You are clearly powerful individuals and can make decisions for yourselves. Come, let us parle. Perhaps we can work with each other."

The goblin began to walk towards Hongi Hika. Even

though his face was frenetic, it was still obvious that he found the idea of negotiating with the enemy insulting. His companion, however, grabbed the captive boy and held a sword to his throat. "Stop now, fool. He taunts you. We have the information we need and must go." They began to back away; but as they did so, the large beast looked again at James. "You. Do you not recognise our prisoner? You should." The cryptic question signalled the end of the confrontation; and all three combatants turned and jogged down the street and around a turn in the road ahead.

Robin Hood did not allow them to stop and think. "We need to go and make sure our friends are safe."

Emma and James could not forget the plight of the captive boy, but they followed the ghosts back to the hotel, up the elevator and into their room. They were quiet when they came in the door and found the rest of their friends still sound asleep. Robin whispered to them to lay down while they could; so, Emma found a space on the bed and James on a couch but neither could sleep.

They dozed fitfully, Kurt's image haunting their dreams.

Four

It seemed like only a few minutes had passed before the ghosts were urging the brother and sister and their friends to wake up again. Robin Hood had hot tea and bread and cheese that he passed around, but they did not spend much longer in the room. The sun was not yet up, but apparently the plan was to sneak out and onto the next train to Berlin. The ghosts believed there was no need to hide their progress any more, from the enemy at least. They were sure that it was obvious where they were heading and that any opposition they were going to face would be in place already. They were invisible as they walked to the train station but the quiet, sleepy feeling in the streets told them that the police alert had been called off, or that any search that was occurring after the café incident was occurring elsewhere. The Berlin station was also calm, and so they approached it as one man leading six children again.

Robin Hood purchased tickets; and before long, they were moving off, heading for Belarus and the town of Brest.

There was a need, of course, to tell those team members that had been sleeping about the happenings of the night before. Leah and Billy were at first angry that they had been left in the hotel room, but Richard and Mabel were more relaxed. All calmed down when Robin gave his reasons; and all were quiet as they listened to a description of the fight and the enemy ghosts that had appeared; and, of course, they were all told about Kurt. Emma and James described the boy, his mannerisms as he was fighting and the pained expression he had as he was being taken away by the enemy.

"He is my cousin." James' voice was almost a whisper. "Don't ask me how I know. I'm sure it involves the added senses we have been given. I also bet that, again, this is no coincidence. Kurt is from Poland and these monsters know I was adopted from there."

King Arthur squeezed his companion's shoulder. "Be at peace, my friend. This, now, becomes a part of our quest. We will not leave the boy."

There was silence for a few minutes as the train rattled smoothly along the tracks. The compartments around them contained two or three passengers but they were behind closed doors, and so the setting was good for a final discussion with the ghosts – listening, learning and preparing for the end of the mission. They had a clearer idea of what awaited them at Brest; and the destination was getting closer, so nerves were beginning to jangle in the bodies of the protectors.

Knowledge, Emma thought, *helps in any situation*, and so she asked another question. "There were two ghosts possessing Kurt and that made you very angry. Why were you so upset?"

There was a frown on King Arthur's face as he spoke. "We have told you; there are ethics even for the dead. Of course, to expect someone who has been solely driven by greed on Earth to follow rules in the Otherworld is perhaps naïve, but there are codes nonetheless. But, it seems like we are at a moment in time when codes mean little. Possession itself rarely happens and is wrong, but possession by two spirits is unheard of. The mind and body are not made for such things and you could see the effect on the poor boy."

Richard had been in quiet discussion with Hippocrates, trying to think how they might use their skills to help. "Hua Mulan, I heard you mention the term 'purgatory' when challenging the enemy. What exactly is purgatory?"

The warrior looked over to Ada Lovelace and nodded. She was so good with detailed explanations. The scientist rubbed her hands together and considered her answer. "Purgatory is a kind of limbo, where troubled souls pass through on their way to the Otherworld. We have talked of a calm existence in the afterlife – an existence which promotes peace. Purgatory is more of a void, a nothingness which suffocates extreme emotions or thoughts. It is not the hellish place of suffering that is described in some religious writing, but no one wants to be there. It is a waystation for evil individuals after death, but, also, if you die twice, that is your penance. Understand, there have not been many examples of paranormal conflicts. We are in a highly unusual period in mankind's history. But it is known; a ghost can't 'kill' a ghost because he or she is already dead, so the ghost does not die. Instead, that ghost goes to purgatory. The fact that our enemy risks purgatory shows that they seek a prize worthy of a monumental gamble."

"It looked like it was difficult for Robin Hood to fight the boy. Is this a tactic that might be used again against us? Billy was thinking ahead and turned back to Ada Lovelace for guidance.

"A ghost cannot kill a person. We have practiced with you in Loxley Chase but if our swords had struck you, they would have had no effect. Robin Hood is different because the power he has gained, the earth essence he has taken on as a guardian of Sherwood Forest, has given him solidity and so he could have harmed the boy – Kurt – which is why he was careful. If we as ghosts are in a human body, we can then use the body to kill, the body we are in can be killed, but we, of course, still cannot die ourselves because we are already dead. Again, purgatory. Does all of this make sense?"

The protectors nodded carefully while absorbing these new ideas, and then Gouyen joined the conversation. She did not speak much, so when she did everyone listened. "You have heard this fact, I know, but I am going to repeat it. Heed its importance. There is dark magic loose in the Otherworld. This has not always been so, but it has been festering in the shadows. This evil is present in the enemy, I feel it. There is a reason this assault is taking place now so we must beware. We do not know what black force has been conjured to match the power of Isanaklesh but we must be alert."

Robin Hood took control again. First, he nodded to Gouyen. "Thank you, my friend. We are lucky to have access to your wisdom on our journey." Gouyen gave a slight bow of her head in response. Then the archer continued in a forceful and clear voice. "The most important point I want to make: you should avoid all fighting if you can. Our goal is to find and retrieve the grail. It is not to conquer the enemy. Secondly, if you do have to fight, you should be careful no matter who it is you are fighting against. In all battles, there are unknown challenges."

King Arthur followed Robin's advice with his own. "I know I should heed my own warning here, because you have all seen my temper get the better of me. Still, I implore you, no matter what happens, stay with your companions. We are stronger together, so if there is a reason why we leave your bodies, stay close. We can enter them again in but a second and we can protect you in many ways, and, my friends, you can protect us. Stay close!"

There was a period of silence as all in the compartment considered what they had heard and then Mabel spoke. "Hongi Hika, would you really have talked with the goblins if they had agreed?"

"I did not ever think they would agree, Mabel. I was probing. In the café, at the train station, we fought ghosts. They were basic foot soldiers for the enemy. These Goblins of Greed are like nothing I have ever seen. I do not know what beings were abused to make these monsters, but it was worth attempting to talk to find out more."

Hua Mulan decided to move the meeting along and focus on the days ahead. "The person I learned most from when I was alive was my father, Fa Zhou. He did not want me to go to war in his place, but he was proud of me nonetheless. He would always say the same thing whenever I came home to visit. 'Planning and preparation, my daughter. You can win any battle with the right planning and preparation.' Ada Lovelace, please help us plan and be prepared."

The scientist reached up and pulled another map from the storage rack above and rolled it out on the floor of the carriage for all to see. "Of course, my general. Gouyen and I have been working together to make sure our team is prepared. Please pay close attention because you are all important to this strategy. Here is the Białowieża Forest or a closeup of that area." The map below them was interesting because it showed a large forest in the centre of the scene, but the forest was surrounded by open scrubland before buildings appeared. Then there was a typical cramped, urban scenario with bars, nightclubs, factories and lots of dark alleys.

"What is that there? Is that the house you mentioned we might head to?" Richard was pointing to a lone structure that stood on the edge of the forest next to what looked like a ruin or pile of rubble.

"You have a sharp pair of eyes, young man. That is the old Białowieża Lodge House, what used to be the servant quarters next to a large mansion. The mansion was bombed during World War II but somehow the lodge house survived. It is uninhabited because it sits too close to the trees and people are afraid of the forest. Our plan is to use that house as a base when we go to look for the grail. Richard and Hippocrates, if there are injuries, we will bring the victims there. Leah, you and I will set up a command centre in the lodge and will direct our efforts from there. When we find the chalice, it will be brought to the base first and then we will plan our escape."

The train continued to speed along the tracks, seemingly faster and faster with Brest in its sights. The quest for the grail was nearing its climax and the protectors continued to feel a level of tension they had not experienced before. James, in particular, was lost in thought, picturing again and again his father back home in Loxley, continuing to link him and his recovery to the health of the planet. He also now had the mystery of Kurt to think about.

"I know this is not the time for this. But I just want to know. We have lost two of the ancient relics. If we cannot stop the enemy from stealing the grail, are we doomed? Will the Earth survive?" James looked from ghost to ghost as he asked the question.

Arthur stood and pulled Excalibur from its scabbard, then he drove it down into the centre of the map. The sword was quivering, but still shining bright, standing straight up, embedded in the floor of the carriage. Even though his actions had been violent, the king was smiling down at James. "Hear me now, ghosts and protectors alike. We will not fail. We will capture the grail and we will secure this old forest and reclaim it for our cause. I swear it on my sword."

All the inhabitants of the carriage stared at Arthur as he pulled Excalibur free from the floor and returned it to its sheath. Of course, nothing was ever certain, but it was hard not to believe words when they were spoken with such conviction.

"We should rest for a while. Sleep if you need to sleep because we are not far from our destination." Robin Hood's voice was quiet, soothing. The protectors curled up, on the floor or in corners of the seats, heads on balled-up coats or leaning back against the cushions. They became lost in their own thoughts, their own ideas, all imagining and preparing in their own way for what was to come. And then sleep finally took them.

The Grail
One

Everyone was used to the train whistle now – its long, shrill note indicating that they were close to their destination; but this whistle was different and caused a lot of deep breaths and racing hearts. The Pachamama Protectors were all looking out of the window and the city they saw was grey and bleak, a concrete mass of sad desolation. It looked as though it was hotter than ever outside, even though the friends had a stereotypical image of countries close to the Baltic Sea being frigid in the winter. People they saw looked irritable, sweating in inappropriate work clothes or because of the sheer number of bodies that jostled them on the streets. The temperature could have been an excuse for grim mindsets, but the friends didn't think it was the weather alone that had dampened the spirits of the population. They did not see anyone talking or laughing or running or playing, just individuals that walked or drove in silence. The skies were drab and overcast and matched a city which was full of plain functional buildings with no colour, no decorations left over from Christmas or flashing lights advertising sweets or drinks or holiday destinations. The weather was clammy, the people and their city were stifled, but King Arthur's voice was cold as he spoke.

"There was a time, in olden days long gone, when

Brest was a bustling town with traders from all over the East and West coming together to swap goods and stories before resuming their journeys to St Petersburg or Rome or Cairo. When the grail arrived, it could have had the same effect on the forest and the surrounding community as Robin Hood and his vessels of power had on Sherwood and Loxley. But, unfortunately, the grail came here with Mordred at a dark time. I had been defeated, my friends slain, and Mordred was determined to hide his new treasure until he could find a way to use it. We now think this was when plans first began in the Otherworld – when evil souls decided they should take the grail. These ghouls began to impose their own influence on Brest, attracting thousands of opportunistic people who settled and grew the city into a hub for gambling, drinking, drugs and fighting. Brest became the capital of the east for all gangsters and thieves, which is so ironic because at its heart lay a symbol of hope, containing all that was good and fertile about Mother Earth. The forest thrives – but be careful, my friends, because we enter a city that is full of mankind's most corrupt and the Otherworld's most opportunistic dark spirits."

King Arthur's last words of warning put the protectors on high alert. They walked off the train and down a dingy platform and immediately began attracting glances and outright stares. It was, of course, because one man led six children and there was no clear reason why six children would be arriving in Brest. Still, they walked on, out of the station and down a main street that was full of liquor stores and convenience stores, selling lottery tickets, cigarettes, beer and fast food. There was music blaring out of bars and drunk or homeless people were sitting propped up against walls or lying in gutters, covered in fluttering plastic bags, bottles and cans. The city really was the most desolate place any of them had ever seen. If it could possibly have become any worse, it did when Gouyen again told Mabel that they were being followed. This time when she walked faster and told Robin Hood, he turned around immediately and stared at a man wearing a long trench coat and old army boots who gave a toothless grin to the group, realising he had been spotted.

Robin Hood spoke quickly. "We are too exposed. I think it would be easy for a fight to begin here in broad daylight. I'm sure brawls are not unusual. Let us abandon the idea of a hotel and go to our final destination, where we can defend ourselves with more certainty." The group hurried down the street and turned a corner at the end.

"Robin, this was not the route Hongi Hika laid out on the map?" Billy relayed a message from his companion in a shaky voice because now they were in a very dark alley that ran between tall buildings and shut out all but a distant, high up strip of dull sky.

Water dripped down the walls and made sludgy, dirty puddles on the path, and rats ran openly between sewer drains.

"I know, but it is a quicker route, and, for now, I prefer speed." At that moment, two men stepped out of the shadows ahead and blocked the path. It was not clear whether they were enemy spies or if they were just regular criminals on the seedy streets of Brest, but whatever they were, it did not matter to Robin Hood. He drew his sword and, in an instant, slashed an arm and skewered a leg, leaving two screaming men on the floor. His friends took this incident in their strides, hopping over the writhing forms and jogging to the end of the alley and out into more noise and smoke.

This next big street was brighter – an open, main thoroughfare teeming with noisy cars that sped by or honked furiously if anything got in their way. Far ahead, between tall buildings, they could see a lone ray of light appearing out of the clouds as the sun tried to force its way free from curtains of smog. The ray hit the ground in the distance at the end of two more dark alleys where, barely distinguishable through the gloom, there was a splash of green colouring. Slowly, the team realised they could smell the fresh, cool aroma of trees and they quickly looked for a way to cross the busy street. A series of yells erupted from behind them and upon turning, Leah saw four brutes standing over the men Robin Hood had wounded. They began shouting louder, pointing in their direction, and then marching furiously towards them. They were in trouble.

Analytical as ever, Ada Lovelace formed a plan and stepped out of Leah's body. She turned herself into a glowing, fluorescent ghoul and then floated off into the street. Two cars passed through her before a third swerved in shock and surprise, ramming into a big truck which, in turn, skidded into a long and wide limousine. There was chaos on the street now but at least the traffic had stopped and so Robin led the protectors on a zigzag path through crashed cars and screaming motorists. Ada Lovelace had slipped straight back into Leah as the mayhem had occurred so it was not clear to the angry drivers why the crash had happened or who they could blame, which meant the protectors made it safely across the street just as the thugs came out of their alley. One of them was waving to a fellow hoodlum, another giant of a man who was on the same side of the street as the protectors but a block down. He quickly grabbed two colleagues and they began to run towards the protectors at speed.

"Robin, we need to get out of here." Mabel was looking straight ahead and then left at converging enemies, then she lost track of them as she and her friends disappeared down another alley, still heading towards the ray of light and the greenery. This pathway was no less dank and murky than their previous route, with garbage and sewage everywhere, but young legs were giving them an advantage as they hopped over obstacles and began to put distance between themselves and their pursuers. Then, suddenly, and shockingly, just as they were about to reach another road ahead, a gunshot rang out and a bullet ricocheted off a window ledge just above Emma's head.

"Okay, that's enough." Robin Hood ushered his companions around a corner, knelt quickly and pulled out his bow and an arrow. The arrow shimmered in the gloom that seemed to cover the whole city. "I wanted to avoid open combat with the living, if possible, but I cannot abide guns, especially guns aimed at children. Let us see what they think of my ancient ways, shall we?" Still out of sight, around a corner, Robin put an arrow in place, pulled back the bow string until it was taut and then with amazing speed, he leaned around the corner, spotted and sighted the gunman and fired. The protectors could not resist themselves even though they knew it was dangerous. Each of them peeked around the corner and saw a big, towering man toppling to the ground with an arrow sticking out of one eye. His fellow thugs had dropped flat on the pathway, lying in dirt and refusing to move because they had no idea what to do when an archer was firing at them. In many ways, it was more frightening than gunfire because it was unexpected. All the criminals stayed low and out of sight, occasionally glancing over at their dead partner who was lying on his back, wearing a shocked expression, skewered by a still glowing piece of yew.

The second road the protectors came to was not as busy as the first and was easier to cross. They carried on running, bending over slightly in case there was any more gunfire, but apparently the arrow had had an impact far beyond the death of one man, and, as James looked back, he could not see any pursuers at all. He stayed quiet however, partly because he needed all of his breath for running and partly because he could feel King Arthur inside of him recommending he focus on escape. There was no telling who else might be tracking them, so the sooner they made it to their safe house, the better. The last alley was long and less used than the previous two, perhaps because it was closer to the forest. Still, it was dingy and dank and Robin Hood and the protectors were pleased to finally make it into an open space. Spotting a small brick house in the distance, everyone began sprinting towards safety. They ran over scrubland and flattened earth covered in old cement slabs and wooden timbers – a wasteland of discarded debris – the result of fear as the old forest had grown and spread.

To Emma and James, the trees that were coming closer

and closer looked inviting, like an oasis after many days of travelling through the desert. This was a primeval forest much like Loxley Wood, full of ancient oaks and yews that had been in that same place for many centuries. They could smell an earthy, sappy scent as they got nearer and it reminded them of home. It was a smell that the people of Loxley had grown used to but that the citizens of Brest found threatening and alien. As Robin and the protectors ran, they felt exposed in the open but somehow safe as the feel of the trees washed over them, and then another, even more primitive feeling hit them, almost stopping them in their tracks. They could sense the grail.

Luckily, Gouyen was looking back and alerted Mabel when two of the enemy soldiers appeared from out of a gap in the buildings, carrying guns. She screamed a warning and the protectors carried on running, keeping low, dodging holes and debris on the ground until, finally, they made it to the door of the old building. The thugs were not following; they were just standing, on the edge where the city stopped and the open scrubland began, watching. The sun had begun dipping down in the sky behind the office blocks and towers, dropping behind grey clouds, and the glow from the end of the day showed Brest in a silhouetted, smoky haze. Robin turned the handle on the door, pushed it open with a loud, old creak and everyone filed into their sanctuary, finally safe for a few hours at least.

Two

The inside was empty of all the trappings of life, no furniture or pictures or carpets on the floor. It was dusty and musty, but otherwise felt surprisingly secure. The door had opened straight into the main living room with what looked like a kitchen off to the right. The walls were red brick inside as well as out, the floors hardwood – not scratched or worn – and there was a big, deep fireplace in the back centre of the room. On the left, a set of stairs led up to the second floor and presumably some bedrooms. All the ghosts stepped free of their protector friends and Gouyen set off immediately up the stairs to explore, taking Hippocrates with her in case the house contained hidden enemy spies and so he could scout out areas that could be used for medical emergencies. The physician felt good about the house. For some reason, it felt like a home even though it clearly hadn't been lived in for centuries.

They were sure they were safe, for the time being at least, and so the remaining ghosts joined in the search, investigating the ground floor and basement. Each of the young friends slumped onto the floor in the main room, backs against the wall. Billy immediately fell asleep with his head on Mabel's shoulder. They had not slept for many hours but had been sustained by the excitement of their journey and by the energy that came from their companions. Gouyen and Hippocrates came back down the stairs and reported that the second floor had three bedrooms and was free of any hidden threats. Robin immediately picked Billy up and beckoned for the protectors to come with him. "If you get some sleep now, you will be stronger in the morning." Richard, Mabel, Billy and Leah followed without question, but Emma and James just stayed on the floor, heads leaning back against the wall.

When Robin was back, he and the rest of the ghosts sat cross-legged in front of the brother and sister. "You are both stubborn. You should get some rest."

"What's it like not to sleep?" James yawned as he asked.

The question made Ada Lovelace laugh. "I did not sleep much in life. It seemed like a waste of valuable time."

"I miss it." Hua Mulan was honest. "It gave me a few hours at least when I did not long for my family."

"I'm not sure any of us will get much sleep tonight." King Arthur stood by a window, watching the sunset and looking for trouble. He had obviously found some and his colleagues jumped up and ran to look.

"Word travels fast." Hongi Hika sounded calm, even though the scene outside was not.

There was activity everywhere they looked – on the scrubland and way back to the edges of the city. It was a mixture of all the bad things they could have imagined seeping from evil Brest. Nearest to the buildings, crowds of men gathered around hastily built bonfires which gave them light and a way to roast meat and warm coffee. Other colleagues stood guard, watching the trees with shotguns in their hands and rifles slung over their shoulders. Robin Hood had clearly killed and injured some key figures in the local mafia because it seemed like every gangster in the city had come out to lay siege to the little brick house by the forest. No individual came too close though. Big tough thugs they may have been, still they were afraid of whatever was in the trees – and whoever was in the house. They were content to wait on the edges of the open land, because whoever had the fancy bows and arrows and kooky friends would need to come out at some point and they planned to be there waiting with much more firepower, enough to overpower an archer and his teenage gang.

The mobsters watched the house, but each one of them regularly cast nervous glances to their left where another, stranger gathering was taking place. The villains and thieves had heard the rumours that the forest was haunted, and if they had not received orders from the godfather himself to stand guard in front of this house, they would have scattered and run for home immediately. The second congregation was closer to the trees, and closer to the house, clearly positioned to stop any retreat to the forest or to the city. It was a flickering, fluorescent, shapeshifting amalgamation of weirdness that illuminated itself and everything that was going on in that small area of scrubland.

"It looks like a reunion party for the ghosts of every criminal, mobster or gestapo member that ever terrorised the common woman or man. And those Goblins of Greed. Look, dozens of them. Every base instinct for destruction sucked up and moulded into one being." Ada Lovelace shivered as she watched.

Robin Hood and his friends joined the vigil at the windows. There were dozens of spectral figures standing and sitting, watching the house, and Ada Lovelace was right. The throng contained greed from every century, plus some extra special creations, designed to provide brute force in the mission to steal nature's power. In addition, in the middle of the group, Emma spotted twenty or more solid, living young people whose bodies rippled slightly in the fading light. The group of teenagers looked angry, fanatical and in pain, but they stayed still, ready and waiting for the signal to fight. On the edge of the huddle of living individuals, she could see Kurt, flexing his hands, waiting to grasp a weapon. At regular intervals, he ran his fingers through his hair and his eyes flicked left and right, as though he was also looking for an opportunity to run.

James turned and stared around the room, a look of panic on his face. "What are we going to do?"

King Arthur spoke first. "Be calm, young James, be calm. Come, let us sit and talk." His expression was relaxed, thoughtful, as though he was now in his element – the time before battle. It was clear that the closeness of war took him into a place of serenity. All the ghosts moved to the middle of the room and sat cross-legged, except for Gouyen who kept watch at the window. She was looking for any signs that could help give them an edge, help them succeed, but she could not stop her eyes from flicking to the assembled enemy ghosts, laughing and gloating at the perceived triumph they felt was coming.

"How can we get the grail and fight off all of those things at the same time?" Emma looked as concerned as her brother but took a deep breath as she saw the confidence on display in front of her. "I guess we should be quiet and just listen, shouldn't we? I'm sure you guys have been in this kind of trouble before."

Robin looked back at the window. "Wise woman. Please join us. Let the outside world be what it will be. We need your story to guide us."

Gouyen came and stood in the middle of the group, folded her arms across her chest and closed her eyes. As she started to speak in a clear but hypnotic voice, Hongi Hika began a rhythmic chant that was almost a whisper. The chant did not contain words but was tonal and mesmerising.

"I no longer remember my birth name. I am Gouyen, Apache woman, sage lady of my tribe. Wife and witness to the murder of my husband. We were hunting together, at one with the wind and sky and prairieland until a Comanche soldier ambushed us and killed my beloved. But not only killed, he took his scalp and left him forever scarred in the Otherworld. My father was old, his father was old, all our men were weak. Still, I craved revenge. I cut my hair in the way of a widow but constructed my mind in the way of a warrior. For what I planned to do, I would be an outcast in the Otherworld because killing in cold blood is wrong. Still, I put on my special outfit, one I had worn before to become a woman and to become a wife. I crept away from my home and, for three days and three nights, walked overland to our enemy's village. Once there, I found the assassin, lured him away from his people and murdered him. Sometimes there are things that need to be done and nothing can stop them being done. This was such a thing and this" – she pointed at the window – "is such a thing. We will succeed."

Gouyen's story was a haunting tale of strength and resolve. Along with Hongi Hika's hypnotic chant and the strength of the trees that they could feel close by, Emma and James felt calm resolve flowing through their veins. They could not yet see the path to victory – the road that would lead them from this house to the grail, back to Loxley and their father, and then to a greener, kinder world; but they knew that they were in the company of a group of wise elders, leaders of men and women through the ages, who would find that path. They were teenagers; they had yet to live their lives, but they could feel that their finest hour was just around the corner, and they were ready.

Three

The ghosts worked out a strategy that was daunting but could work. They fine-tuned every detail and then Emma and James slept a little while Gouyen continued to watch the enemy outside, both living and dead. Hongi Hika put the finishing touches to a new bow he had made from Sherwood Forest wood and Hua Mulan polished her shining, curved sword and then just before dawn, Ada Lovelace went up to the bedrooms and woke the sleeping protectors. After a few yawning minutes, as they tried to figure out where they were, they came downstairs, sat in the middle of the living room and focused. They knew they needed to be attentive as their king, with Excalibur drawn and ready, went over each aspect of the plan again. There were some simple tactics that relied on the experience of all, and some more hopeful schemes that relied on the strength and power of a few, but there was a plan.

"Leah and Ada Lovelace will rout the gangsters and their guards at first light. We have all experienced the panic of war. These men are afraid enough already, looking at a troop of ghosts while trying to sleep, laying in the shadows of a daunting forest. We will just add the right spark that will ignite this fear. I am not concerned about the hoodlums of Brest. I am more concerned about the dead and the young boys they have ensnared."

"Our enemies are many and we are few, but we have

what they do not have." Arthur did not need to spell out what their greatest assets were; he just looked from face to face, from Hua Mulan to Robin Hood, from Ada Lovelace to Hongi Hika, from Gouyen to Hippocrates and then to the young protectors. "And I do not just mean the wise and brave ghosts we have assembled. I mean you also." He pointed at each of the children. "History has been made again and again by young people willing to fight for a cause and we have a mighty cause."

"Our strategy is simple. We will hold our enemy, fight our enemy and when the time is right, Emma and James will leave us for the forest. They have been our leaders all along. They must complete the final stage of our quest. Gouyen can feel that it needs to be a young Pachamama Protector who retrieves the grail. We believe if Emma and James can come out of the trees with the cup, our enemy will be daunted, and we can escape this place and leave quickly for England. Mabel, you and Gouyen will be our tacticians. Things will change and we need two practiced eyes to help us switch our approach if that is needed."

There were questions and answers, and points were made clearer. The discussion was a good one but was cut short by a warning from Gouyen. Her sharp eyes could begin to see a hint of light in the sky. Sunrise was coming and gloom was needed to add to the surprise attack on the criminals. Ada Lovelace had a cloth bag over her shoulder when the ghost stepped into Leah. There was no ceremony, no last words or hugs. Leah just slipped out of a side door and began to take a wide route away from the enemy ghosts but around and back to a set of buildings on the edge of the city. Her friends did not watch her go, but, in the house, they prepared themselves, because they knew that they were minutes away from going out of the front door and when they did that, the battle would truly begin.

Leah was pleased with herself. She was agile, but sneaking through the rubble and refuse quietly when there was an enemy horde close by was no small feat. She continued to wind her way through the dark until she was less than twenty metres from the edge of the camp. The thugs had clearly become bored and tired overnight. Many of them slept and those that had been put on guard were yawning with droopy eyes and faraway looks on their faces. Ada Lovelace came out from her friend's body and then, with Leah following, she crept around the base of a tall office building that stood next to the sleeping men – men who were sprawled next to the shimmering embers of fires from the night before. The scientist had worked on a series of ghostly scientific devices with Hippocrates that evening and was now laying them on the ground at intervals. When they had made a complete circuit of the office block, Ada Lovelace gave Leah a small amulet and then whispered instructions to her. The girl nodded, indicating that she understood; and so, the ghost crept around the back of the camp, unseen, behind more buildings until she was on the opposite side of Leah. Taking a deep breath and counting to three, she then began the first stage of King Arthur's plan.

The sleeping thugs and mafia henchmen woke to an out of this world wailing; and looking to one side of the camp, they saw a ten-foot-tall ghost walking towards them, waving its hands in the air. Seconds later, there was a loud bang on the other side of their site and an office building erupted, engulfed in shimmering silver flames. If that wasn't enough to cause panic, glowing arrows of death started flying from the windows of the house they had been watching, hitting the standing guards before they could react or think of retaliation. Arthur had been right. In battle, confusion often equalled panic, especially when the individuals involved were not motivated. The tired and scared thugs realised they were not getting paid very much to do what they were doing and were facing supernatural foes, so they ran en masse back into the city, leaving behind guns, supplies and quite a few wounded colleagues.

The enemy encampment of ghouls was not affected by panic, of course. They were surprised by the chaos behind them but flaming buildings and silvery arrows did not scare them. They just saw it as a signal for action and everyone came to their feet, ready to do battle. King Arthur had known this, of course, and the next part of the plan was just to fight with more vigour and passion than the enemy could muster. Robin Hood had fired six arrows at the thugs and when the sixth had been unleashed, the protectors raced out of the front door and stood in a line, ready to meet a charge of evildoers. Hongi Hika then set loose six more arrows from his newly made bow, taking down several ghosts before the bulk of the enemy arrived and then they were in the middle of pandemonium.

The instructions given to the protectors had been simple. In battle, they should not worry about enemy ghouls because the ghouls could not harm them. They could defeat their companion ghosts and send them to purgatory, of course; but they could not inflict harm on the living. The bulk of the bad spirits were there to try and outnumber the legends, to inflict damage if there was confusion caused by sheer numbers, but also to scare the young boys and girls. They were fortune hunters, and it made no difference to them if they lost and were in purgatory or the darkest reaches of the Otherworld. Their only hope to avoid endless pain somewhere in the afterlife was to win. Ideally, for Robin Hood and his friends, the ghouls would be dispatched quickly because the legends were better fighters. The friends had been told to worry about the captured teenagers who were possessed. They could do harm to child and ghost alike and needed to be handled carefully. But, also, of course, they were innocent victims; and so, if possible, they needed to be spared.

There were so many enemies though; it was hard to be tactical and thoughtful. King Arthur and Hua Mulan stayed inside James and Emma and fought in the front row with Robin Hood. Richard and Billy with Hippocrates and Hongi Hika as their internal companions were in the second row, stabbing and parrying from behind. It was an old shield-wall theory from the past that King Arthur had used in battle and was designed to put one set of warriors at the front to fight face-to-face, with another group of fighters behind to do damage through the gaps in the wall. This, of course, was a pitifully small shield wall, but the lack of size was made up for by the stature of the men and women who were fighting. Working from inside of his young friend, King Arthur had turned James into a knighted champion of old. With a fire in his heart, he whirled his bang staff around and about and through the air with a fury that was deadly. Evil ghosts were sucked into limbo left and right as he fought. The more renowned ghouls kept clear of that deadly stick, knowing it was a conduit for the mighty Excalibur. Emma, too, was a formidable foe with the frenzied Hua Mulan inside her. The warrior general had channelled all her considerable skill into the slim arms of a young girl and now Emma was making ghosts from all time periods pay, slashing and stabbing and causing explosions of smoke left and right as purgatory gained more evil souls. And then there was Hongi Hika, creating a Māori warrior out of Billy, using fists, feet and the bang staff to down criminals in any way possible.

Robin Hood was also formidable. He had a cause again and fought for the grail because it would restore Sherwood Forest to its former glory and planet Earth to its former glory, which, in turn, would turn evil aside. He fought for a second chance for mankind and so he fought with a burning passion. Richard was not really a fighter and, of course, had a physician as his companion, but he had saved some of the special devices that had routed the mafia, which meant he could lob silvery bombs into the crowd, dispatching ghosts three or four at a time.

The plan could not have been going any better until the possessed teenagers appeared at the front of the enemy ranks. Then the swordplay of the legends needed to be more careful, thoughtful – the frenzied passion was lost. As they fought, the protectors could see torn expressions on the faces of the captured boys and it was a sickening sight. At one moment, their faces showed evil abandon – laughing malevolence that made the young men terrifying to behold – and then just briefly there was a look of pain or fear that came straight from the hearts of boys. It looked like the enemy had been no less cruel this time than the last time they had met. It appeared there were at least two ghosts in each teenager causing mental and physical agony to each child.

The battle began to turn against them and that was when Hua Mulan made a decision – a decision that Emma did not like. The Chinese warrior mentally rebuked the girl. "This is war, my young friend; no time to question me. In battle, we do what we must do and beg forgiveness when the war is over. Do as I say."

Emma knew she was right and so she relayed a message to Leah and then turned back to the fight and immediately slashed at a young boy's leg. The captive howled in pain; and as he crashed to the floor, two ghouls appeared and James and King Arthur savagely hacked them into oblivion. Leah then reluctantly stabbed another boy in the thigh; and as he collapsed, the ghosts of two more brutes were speared in the chest by Billy and Hongi Hika. Two simple, if ruthless, actions had changed the makeup of the contest and caused hesitancy in the enemy ranks. When Robin Hood dispatched three more ghosts with one slash of his sword, he looked at James and nodded, then he did the same thing to Emma. Immediately, King Arthur and Hua Mulan became ghosts again, joined in with the battle and the brother and sister began sprinting towards the forest, sensing, feeling the grail and victory in their grasp.

Four

Gouyen and Mabel were still in the house, continuing to assess the battle. The Apache leader had told them all before the fighting started that a plan was only perfect when drawn in the sand. Put into practice, a plan was flawed because it was subject to the anomalies and actions of the opposing fighters and so it needed to be changed and changed again. Up until that point, she had been surprised by the effectiveness of this strategy, but just as she had begun to hope that their luck would hold, the first crack appeared and it was a crack that became a giant hole. They had watched as Emma and Leah slashed and poked at the boys' legs and Gouyen had silently congratulated Hua Mulan on her decision. The boys would be hurt, but, if all went well, Hippocrates and Richard could patch up their wounds. They then watched as Emma and James turned and began to run towards the forest. Mabel and Gouyen urged them on with anxious looks on their faces and then, from out of nowhere, their worst nightmares appeared.

From behind the house, four ghosts came into view; and more than any others they had seen so far, these spirits oozed contempt and gluttony. Each of them was a Goblin of Greed on steroids, an amalgamation of multiple evil spirits into one beast. Gouyen recognised them as the kind of men who had raped and pillaged her ancestral lands. She knew the same thing had been done on every continent, meaning Mother Earth had found herself parched and barren or covered in concrete jungles rather than living, breathing, green jungles. These apparitions were big – tall and wide – and, like the previous goblins they had seen, had psychotic expressions. They looked to Mabel like video game monsters – multiple eyes, noses and slavering mouths that were filled with teeth.

So intent were Emma and James on making it to the forest that they did not see the beasts coming, and by the time they did, it was too late. Two of the ghouls flew straight into James' body, one disappeared into Emma and the final goblin took up a defensive stance. Their thinking was clear – the possession would happen quickly and they could use James to battle the legendary ghosts while Emma retrieved the grail. Their assumptions were wrong in many ways.

It was a testament to the strength and passion of the brother and sister that any kind of struggle occurred against the goblins.

Gouyen, now running out of the house to help, believed in the children, but even she wondered if the ghouls' tactic might not succeed. The possessors were evil beings and enemy leaders and the fact that they had decided to occupy James and Emma showed how important they thought the two members of the protectors were. It was only as she got close that Gouyen realised Mabel was following her and, in fact, was overtaking her. At the last moment, the ghost dived into the girl to try and protect her and managed to slow her down so that she could shout a warning back to their battling colleagues. It wasn't needed, however, because Robin Hood had also seen the trouble and had dispatched the last visible goblin with two well-placed arrows. Now all the protectors had abandoned the battle and were running to help. Emma was heading for the forest and James had turned to fight his former friends. It was clear that the enemy had been clever, that they were trying to seize the grail for themselves while also causing maximum chaos in their enemy's ranks. The thought of Emma and James being possessed was causing turmoil in the minds of both the protectors and their legendary friends.

Mabel was as distressed as everyone, particularly at the sight of her best friend in peril; and despite Gouyen's protests, she was the closest to the forest so she changed direction to chase after Emma. As she did this, James turned her way. The look on the boy's face was the most frightening thing she had ever seen. The expression showed what kind of battle was going on in his mind, body and soul – anger and horror mingled with hatred and glee. Mabel and Gouyen were too disoriented by everything that was happening to do anything but put up the most basic defence as James brought his bang staff crashing down on the girl's own weapon, driving it back onto her head. There were shouts of horror from the running protectors but not a sound from Mabel as she slumped to the ground. James stood over the body and let out a loud and long howl that contained triumph and despair in one drawn out shriek.

Some of the most seasoned veterans of war were on the battlefield to hear that sound. King Arthur, Hua Mulan, Robin Hood, Gouyen and Hongi Hika each had split-second decisions to make and when they made them, it seemed as though they had made them in unison although no communication took place. Gouyen stayed with Mabel to keep her safe. She was groaning lightly but her heartbeat seemed strong. Hongi Hika stayed inside Billy, also to keep him safe, but turned and began to fight the ghosts from the battleground who had followed thinking victory was theirs. Robin Hood fired three quick arrows into the legs of a group of remaining captured teenagers, sending them screaming to the ground and unleashing their ghosts into the fight. He then joined Hongi Hika and Billy with his sword, keeping the massed ranks of the enemy at bay, buying time for Hua Mulan and Arthur. Both the king and general had not hesitated either. They both realised they needed to become companions again to regain control of the bodies and souls of their friends. Hua Mulan flew through the air and straight into the back of Emma, sending her down to the ground with the impact. King Arthur did not need to fly, only to run and barge his way into James' body, making the boy freeze for a second – but just a second. He then continued on, forcing his legs forward towards the remaining fight, focusing in on Robin Hood's back as the archer fought determinedly against a wave of enemy ghosts.

Emma was also walking stiffly, reluctantly away towards the forest, her legs rigid and in turmoil like her brother's. Also, like her brother, her face was a complex mask of emotions – anger, fury, exhaustion and determination flickering across her features. All of a sudden, a roar came out of her mouth – a roar of misogynistic frustration and rage. "You do not belong here, geisha girl! We know who you are. Get back to the village and cook for your men."

Emma clutched at her chest, bent over double then stood and began walking again towards the forest. "Stop fighting, Hua Mulan. Join us. There will be plenty of ways for you to help us rule in the Otherworld once we have the grail." This time the voice that came from Emma's mouth was oily, enticing. The multiple presences in the goblin were working individually to try and defeat the Chinese warrior, employing psychology and strength.

Their confidence was misplaced, however. None of the ghouls had bargained for the unusual level of strength that existed in the two women they now fought. Hua Mulan was furious with herself for not protecting Emma. She saw so much of herself in the teenager – a desire to protect her family and a passion to make a difference in the world despite the odds. She was also furious with the fiends that now sought to possess a young girl, destroy a young girl after they had used her for their own ends. Hua Mulan could feel the stress on Emma's mind and body, but she could also feel a wealth of hidden strength in this remarkable girl. If the warrior had been alone, she might have considered failure and would have realised that she could not break free of this potent possession unaided. But she was not alone and she had no need to be negative, to consider loss. With her own tried and tested heart and the strength of a teenage fighter on her side, she knew she could win.

Emma stopped walking once more and she began to shake. Her fists clenched and her head leaned back and then she let out a mighty scream. "I am a woman of power; this girl is a woman of power. We will not be controlled;

we will not be bullied. We will win!"

The scream turned into a roar and three separated ghouls – sticky and slimy individuals who had once made up the goblin – came tumbling out of the girl. Hua Mulan did not miss a beat and screamed, "Robin Hood", and the Earl of Loxley, marksman extraordinaire, did not hesitate either even though he was in the middle of his own battle. He chopped down a ghost, dropped his sword, flipped his bow off of his shoulder and fired three arrows in succession that fatally struck each enemy phantom – two in the chest and one in the eye.

The ghouls disappeared in a puff of smoke.

Hua Mulan looked around for Emma and saw her lying unconscious in the dust and then looked for her brother. James was walking painfully towards Robin Hood with a sneer and a frown on his face. The archer dropped his bow and picked up his sword once more, just in time to block a blow from the boy. The fight on the outside for James was half-hearted, the real fight was occurring on the inside where a legend and two goblins fought for control of a boy who was strong and who carried the fate of a father and a world in his heart.

Hua Mulan ran over to Mabel and Gouyen. The girl was sitting up groggily, recovering after the blow from James. Reluctantly taking her eyes off of the fight, the Chinese warrior knelt down. "Now is your moment, young lady. Gouyen and I must join this struggle. The battle goes poorly and I sense that despair is not far away. You are the only one left who can claim the grail. Trust that we will keep your new friends safe. Go now, into the trees."

A look of determination appeared in Mabel's eyes as

Hua Mulan left them. She turned to Gouyen who spoke quietly. "Yes, my sister. Now is the time. You have all you need to save us and the world." She grasped one of Mabel's hands, kissed it and then took a small copper ring from her own finger and slipped it onto the girl's. "Now fly." She watched her companion run quickly to the forest alone and saw her swallowed into ancient trees that had not welcomed a man, woman or child for many years. She watched for a few seconds more, even after there were nothing but swaying branches to watch, and then turned back and ran to Robin Hood's side to see where she might be of help in battle.

Five

It was hard for Robin Hood to see how they might win this fight now. He was an optimistic man, but the odds were heavily stacked against them. Leah had made it back from her guerilla excursion against the gangsters and now employed a fighting style that was crude but effective – hacking and scything with her bang staff – showing why her ghost was a scientist and not a fighter. Hua Mulan was as ferocious with a blade as any person the woodsman had witnessed, and she wielded it like a wand, dispatching ghosts in threes and fours. Hongi Hika had Billy using every weapon at his disposal – hands, feet, a knife, a sword. Richard and Hippocrates had crawled to the edge of the fight and were trying to revive Emma. And Robin Hood could not help anyone else in any way, because he was fully focused on James.

While there were times when fighting the boy was an easy task, because King Arthur was inside him – battling furiously against formidable foes which was distracting his companion – there were other times when one of the goblins took hold of James' mind and the boy threw everything at the archer. Robin Hood could cripple James, of course, in the way they had with the captured Polish teens – breaking a leg with a quick slash of the sword – but he just couldn't bring himself to do it. This was James Trueman after all; and, possessed or not, he was their friend and ally. So, Robin fought carefully, thinking all the time, trying to come up with a strategy to win this war or at least prolong it to give Mabel time in the forest.

The turning point came when things looked most bleak. The battle had become so intense that Leah did not see Kurt – the captured boy – break away to outflank her with a malevolent smile on his face. She did see him eventually, but only at the last second, as he looked to bring his sword crashing down on her side. She had parried the blow slightly but still it cut into her arm and the girl let out a loud cry of pain and fell to the floor. Ada Lovelace left her companion at the same time as Kurt's possessors discarded the boy and suddenly two enemy spirits were face to face with the scientist. Both the ghouls grinned malevolently as they realised they were about to fight a woman who was also a mathematician. Arrogant confidence radiated as they advanced to end an insignificant contest. Ada Lovelace, mathematician or not, was determined to stand her ground to protect Leah.

A bigger distraction, however, came from behind the backs of the ghouls and made them freeze. James had seen the fall of Leah – his friend – and what James saw, of course, King Arthur saw and it was too much for the great warrior. He had watched as Emma and James had been possessed, had been helpless as Mabel had run alone into the trees and now he had to see another young protector, who had trusted him, bludgeoned by evil. He needed to help and the only way he could think to help involved forfeiting his own freedom. Somehow, Robin Hood could sense what Arthur was doing though the king was still hidden in James' body. He could sense it in the way James' body suddenly twitched, in the way he dropped his sword and in the sounds he heard – sounds that became screams that filled the open space between the city and the forest. It was the howl of two powerful souls – Goblins of Greed – being throttled, crushed and dragged into the abyss. King Arthur had somehow taken control of two evil spirits, two oppressors who had been supremely confident in their superiority over this ragged group of women, children and ancient men; he had taken control of them with strength of will and passion alone, and when he had them where he needed them, he had committed the ultimate sacrifice. With an explosion of ghostly force that sent all on the battlefield to the ground, he had banished the evil spectres into the depths of purgatory but, in doing so, he also banished himself into that place for imprisoned souls.

There was a moment of stunned silence on the open land – a moment when only the birds could be heard flying away, when only the wind could be heard rustling branches and leaves. It could have been a victorious moment. The most malicious of their enemies had been vanquished. But the cost had been too much to pay. Leah was writhing in pain, holding her arm; James was motionless on his back, ten feet from where his sister lay; Mabel had gone into the forest on her own; and, of course, they had lost one of their most valuable weapons in this war because King Arthur had banished himself to oblivion. Robin Hood felt for a moment like giving up but instead surged to his own feet and called on Richard and Billy for help. Robin carefully picked up James' body, Billy supported Leah under her good arm, then Richard knelt to lift up Emma so they could all retreat to the house. They needed time to recover just as the enemy was regrouping. The ghouls sensed victory at last.

The Horror of Mordred
One

Mabel heard loud screams and howls from behind her but knew that her role in this quest now lay ahead, that finding the grail would be the best thing she could do to rescue this mission. She was conscious that she probably shouldn't be the one to be responsible for this final, important act. She and her family were newcomers to Loxley and she was the newest member of this group of friends. But she had been so affected by the kindness she had found in the village and then the wonders of Loxley Chase that she felt she finally belonged. Gouyen had told her she would be needed – and now she was really needed. She had to be strong. She had to find the grail. The horrors she had left behind were frightening – possessed and wounded friends, ghouls everywhere, her Pachamama Protectors all fighting for their lives. But she felt strangely calm and guided.

The forest she was in was not unlike Loxley Chase. It had an ancient, whispering wisdom in the air. Mabel could also feel the same radiating power that she had experienced coming from Robin Hood's staff and from Excalibur. It was in the breezes that blew through the trees, a soundless pulse that Mabel now followed, weaving as quickly as she could, dodging overhanging branches in the air and roots and bushes on the ground. She broke into a run but did not seem to expend any energy and then, suddenly, up ahead she saw a glow – faint at first but growing brighter and brighter as she drew closer. The glow was behind a thick stand of trees and she ducked and walked through what seemed like a natural entrance and finally stood in a wide clearing.

She felt an overwhelming sense of déjà vu as she looked around, because she could now easily have been standing in Loxley Chase. The clearing was almost exactly the same as the one that they had found in their own wood – where they had first met Robin Hood. It was uniformly round, a small amphitheatre that stretched up to the sky where branches folded over but left room for sunlight or moonlight to poke through. The only difference she could see was that the old tree in the corner was not an oak. It was giant but tall – not round like the Major Oak. Mabel remembered the name from her environment class. It was a Karri Knight tree and her neck hurt as she looked up to try and see the top.

The other change in the space involved the fallen logs, which had been arranged carefully in a circle around a central mound of earth and leaves. Through that mound, a glow shone and a vibration rolled out – the sensation she had been following. They were gentle waves that made tears come to her eyes and caused fear and worry to flow away from her heart, leaving it clean and hopeful. She walked to the centre of the clearing and sat on a log, staring at the glow. She knew she needed to hurry but also realised that haste was not important, that all pain would be washed away at any moment – as soon as she brushed off some leaves and cleared away some earth. The culmination of the quest was here and she needed to breathe it in for just a moment.

Eventually, she knelt and pushed aside the accumulated debris, dug away a layer of dirt that was not thick or deep but was enough to cover a dark metal case. She reached down and pulled at the container. It was heavy but, somehow, she found the strength to drag it out into view. She sat it on the side of the shallow hole she had now made and stared. The case was a dull grey, scratched and dented in places. She knew that this was the lead that had been found in Africa and had been moulded into a carrier for the grail. On the side, there was a crude clasp and she reached her fingers slowly down, fiddled with it until it unfastened and then pushed the two sides of the container until it opened. There – in the heart of a deep black crevice – sat a simple thing of beauty.

The grail was a wide cup, almost a bowl, with a long thin stem that expanded gently before meeting its base. It was made of silver but other than that it was plain, not jewel-encrusted or covered in patterns or words. It was a thin, smooth metal – a vessel that was unblemished – unaffected by any liquid it may have held or by the rough metal that had confined it for hundreds of years. It was perfect and pure; and Mabel had no hesitation in reaching into the container to pick up the cup, holding it in two hands carefully and respectfully. Once she had it, she couldn't resist, needed to lift it to her lips to deliver a gentle kiss to its rim, feeling relief that their quest was nearly over and hoping above hope that this vessel could help them now deliver the world from despair. With the grail in her hands, she felt a quick electric jolt. The sensation encapsulated a victorious moment, the moment they had all been praying for – for themselves, for the natural world and for Emma's father who now surely would return to full health.

And then she heard a footstep behind her. She turned quickly, hoping beyond hope that it was Gouyen who had followed her, had followed her after helping to defeat the enemy. But the figure that stood at the edge of the clearing was not Gouyen; it was not her newly discovered soulmate; it was not a person to share in her joy. The figure that stood at the edge of the clearing was a spectre more horrific than she could imagine. It was only partly a man; it was a ghost but only partly a ghost. His image had been eaten away, decayed like a rotting corpse or like the worst depiction of a Hollywood zombie. Half of his face was in tatters with yellowing, blackened teeth showing through the hanging flaps of his cheek. His clothes hung in strips and through the strips of a shirt and leggings, his limbs were made up of part flesh and part bone. He was a nightmare – a nightmare that horrified Mabel, even more so as she realised she could not move; she was frozen in shock.

"It's Mabel, isn't it? I wondered which boy or girl would make it to the end. I thought it would be Arthur's pet, the dying man's son. Or the geisha girl's plaything. But, no, it's the daughter of slaves – the refugee." The ghost's words were slurred and raspy, the sounds whistling through a rotten throat and mouth. "You children have always been key to our plan, as you were key to our enemies' plans – the plans of that egotistical archer and my half-brother. He is King Arthur in name but no true king. Just a thief who stole my crown."

Mabel's mind was whirring, though her body was still locked – through fear or some form of magic. Even though the forest itself still vibrated with goodness and power, the apparition had his own strength and had ensnared her with it. She still had the grail in her hands but could not move. She listened to the phantom's words and a realisation came to her with sudden and appalling clarity. This was Mordred. The ghost of Mordred had returned or had perhaps never left but had been in hiding, had been waiting for centuries to find a way to reclaim his prize – the grail.

"I hear you thinking, young lady. You are bright. Yes, my friends came to the same realisation as your friends, that living youth, existing passion for our planet, was needed to claim and use this vessel – the grail. Great wizards created the other artefacts, but they can be wielded by anyone who is strong and true. The grail, however, was already a mystical thing when Joseph of Arimathea infused it with earth power. Remember the prophecy of old. 'Only the best knight in the land can claim the grail.' So, now, that is you and your friends. What are you called again? 'The Pachamama Protectors.' You are now the best knights in the land! Well done! We, of course, have no people of purity in our army. We have a legion that has been built to do one thing – conquer the Otherworld, the same way we once conquered weak-hearted people on this weak-hearted planet." Mordred's face was hideous, but his expression became increasingly deranged as he spoke.

"Yes, your elders fashioned the artefacts, but our elders are a little different. We have always needed young, vibrant servants, full of life, to carry these earth power vessels. We trapped two young souls – a boy and a girl –

to help us steal the spear and the axe. They are your kin, Mabel. Yours and your friend Emma's. They are now safe in a dark corner of the astral plane. And you, my new young friend, will soon join them. You will be the slave that carries the grail. You will be the tipping point to doom this insipid green planet, allowing us to conquer and control the astral plane, turning it from the Otherworld into our playworld."

Mabel knew that she had to do something. She was not sure what difference it would make because she was alone in the forest and her friends had their own troubles – their own fight to win. But she needed to do something, so she tried to relax, to think and, at the very least, to not give in. What had Gouyen given her when they first met? She said she had given everyone a gift but had given Mabel a little extra. She relaxed some more and began searching inside herself. And while she did, she also tried to keep Mordred occupied. "How did you die?" she asked. "You made it all the way to this forest. What killed you in the end?"

"Do you think I could leave the chalice? Once I had it, once I had succeeded where so many others had failed and I had found the grail, or more appropriately had stolen it from those feeble Knights of the Round Table, I just needed time, to think of how best to wield its power." Mabel realised that Mordred had lost his mind, either while he was alive or after he had become a ghost. The look on his face made him appear more and more unhinged. "I stayed here to scheme, though my legs gave way and my flesh decayed, I stayed, because I knew that one day another quest would come. More do-gooder knights would strive to find the grail. And then this world began to weaken, its power began to seep away and new friends came to me with an idea. They told me that Robin of Loxley was a protector of Sherwood Forest, using the power of the earth; so, they made me a protector of the grail, using the power of Hades. Then they came again and told me Robin Hood had a plan to find the grail so he could use it to save the world and my friends suggested we might steal the idea – and steal their children – and use the grail to power the Underworld."

The ghost's grin continued to widen and he took a step towards Mabel, picturing how he should capture her, how he would begin to possess her so that the grail would finally be his – carried in his arms, or in the arms of a girl he possessed, this time outside of a lead box. He took another step towards her, and Mabel continued to search inside herself to feel for Gouyen's gift. She gripped the grail tightly and kept trying to relax. She thought of the elemental power she had felt in Loxley Wood – the power of the earth they were trying to save and the power of the grail in her hands. She thought of Robin Hood, King Arthur, Hua Mulan – so many legends – her best friend Emma and her newly discovered spiritual sister, Gouyen. How lucky had she been to have found them. Then Mordred's decaying hand touched hers, his fingers began to push themselves into hers. The ghoul leaned forward as though to kiss her with his rotting lips and face but really because he wanted to force his way into her body and soul, to take over her and use her as a tool to destroy her friends, her family, her world. And then his fingers touched a small copper ring.

A glorious silver light filled the enclosure, dazzling

her eyes but not Mordred's because he had his back to the vision and his eyes closed in anticipation of possessing the grail. The light was followed by a deep, perfect voice that made Mabel's heart sing and caused the grail to grow warm in her hands. "Ah, Mordred, fate is a wonderful thing. In death, I have the opportunity to do what I should have done in life."

Mordred broke away from Mabel in terror and turned towards the sound of the voice – the voice of his half-brother – a sound he had hoped never to hear again. He looked into the eyes of King Arthur and realised that his long-held dream of wielding the power of the grail was at an end along with his fantasy of conquering the Otherworld. He realised this even before he saw the flashing light that was Excalibur, scything through the air to send him to purgatory where he would spend an eternity wallowing in regret.

Mabel was on her knees, crying with relief – stunned that she had been saved seconds before being possessed by Mordred. Then the small copper ring on her finger throbbed and she had a revelation. "Arthur, you were lost to us. You sacrificed yourself and went to purgatory. How could you return so quickly?"

Tears continued to flow and King Arthur knelt down and put his arms around the girl. "Be at peace, Mabel. It was you that saved me. You and your adopted sister saved me and saved the world. You are correct. I should not have been able to return. But I felt a pull on my soul, sensed a power like no other take a hold of me and I was transported here. That power was you, Mabel – your bravery, mixed with the enchanted gift Gouyen gave you, mixed with the magic of the earth and the grail. What a potent brew!"

Even though she was overcome with emotion, it was not lost on Mabel that Arthur deserved to be the one to vanquish the murderer and thief Mordred and that it was magic and also fate that had brought him there. She pulled herself away from his arms, looked up at a shining vision in bright armour and lifted the grail, offering it to him as a gift – a thank you for saving her life and for saving the world.

"No, Mabel. Only you can carry the grail. Bring it now, safely in your arms, so we can help our friends and then finish this quest. We will celebrate when we are back in Sherwood Forest itself." Tears still blurred Mabel's vision, but, as she stared into the eyes of the king, she realised, suddenly, he had not come alone.

Two

It was clear that the small stone house on the edge of the forest would provide the illusion of safety and security but only for a while. Solid walls, after all, were no match for the average ghost. They might keep the possessed Kurt and his cohort at bay initially, but even they would find a solution to the temporary standoff, especially with an overwhelming number of ghouls to help. Still, the protectors had time, at least, to care for their wounded, quench their ravenous thirsts and ponder on how close they had come to victory. And they still had Mabel in the woods, though the fact that she was alone scared Robin Hood. She was a resourceful young woman, and Gouyen had seen something special in her which meant a lot, but Robin had an idea that their enemies would not just have massed their ranks outside of the trees but would have had some form of security inside also. His hope had been to have James alongside his sister when searching for the grail. Gouyen had been adamant it needed to be a child that retrieved the cup and the brother and sister together may have stood the best chance of success. But, now, they both lay unconscious on the floor of the cottage, gravely ill, two of three fallen warriors. It was the siblings that concerned Hippocrates and Richard the most, though.

Leah's wound had been bandaged and the bleeding stopped. She had a nasty gash that ran the length of her arm, but the injury had been thoroughly covered in yarrow leaves and she and the other young protectors were now drinking a tea made from the plant. James and Emma's injuries were not as easy to diagnose or heal, however. Hippocrates thought they had some sort of concussion, though of course he had never treated an internal blast – a spiritual explosion that had left the brother and sister lifeless except for some very shallow breathing. Before they had set out on their quest, the Greek physician had had time to scout out plants and bushes with Richard and, luckily, along with the yarrow, he had found several gingko trees growing on the outskirts of Sherwood Forest.

Hippocrates had crushed the leaves and made a drink for James and Emma which he now dribbled gently between their lips. The gingko had been very effective in treating brain injuries in the Peloponnesian War and he hoped it might have the same healing effects now, though this trauma was different than any sword or shield blows he had seen.

While the two medics focused on their unconscious friends, the remaining battle-ready Pachamama Protectors – Leah and Billy – along with the companion ghosts, stared out of a window at the regrouping enemy. The ghouls had lost some important leaders in their army but did not seem to be a sentimental outfit. They wanted victory at any cost and other Goblins of Greed had been created and stepped to the front of the army alongside several returning, living members of the mafia, who must have been paid more than their fear was worth to fight. One goblin seemed to have taken over as the key general in charge. He had formed his soldiers into two lines –

ghouls at the front and gangsters and possessed boys behind – and he looked to be planning an assault on the house. He recognised the ineffectiveness of walls and solid structures when it came to holding off spirits but also the limitation of spirits when it came to damaging buildings or killing the living. He wanted his ghouls to cause as much chaos as possible, battling the enemy ghosts, allowing his solid soldiers to take advantage and enter the house. To that end, a struggling Kurt was brought forward by two burly criminals, and the Goblin of Greed immediately possessed the young Polish boy. The same happened to four other teens.

"We need to barricade the door. If the spirits enter, we can fight them and the protectors are safe, but if the possessed enter then they can harm our young friends." Ada Lovelace realised she was not a fighter and so was trying to think of anything, any way she could help in this situation. There was no furniture in the house, but Richard had found a plank of wood and was trying to wedge it under the door handle. The mathematician looked up and saw the light bulb in the middle of the ceiling then she looked down to the switch that was next to the door. Leah was helping despite her arm, so she tried the light. When it came on, Ada Lovelace asked Billy to run up the stairs to look for any loose electrical wires.

"Here they come." Robin Hood made the announcement and then drew his sword so that he was ready to fight one last time.

There looked to be about fifty ghosts alongside the Polish boys, and he knew that even with such valiant colleagues at his side, there was no way they could hold off this army now – not with the injured children to protect also. For a second, he felt a measure of despair and shame in his heart. Why had he brought these innocents on such a reckless mission? But then his mind went back to Loxley Chase and the pleasure he had felt preparing with his young protectors in the safety and solitude of that ancient wood. And he thought of Emma and James and their father, the green earth they fought for and of the courage of Mabel searching for the grail.

Despair was quickly replaced by contentment and battle readiness. They had tried for the right reasons and if they were to fail now, they would fail in the right way. Robin Hood kissed his sword and watched as the ranks of evildoers came closer and then Kurt, rippling and grimacing, broke away to step forward on his own.

"Robin Hood! I know you are in there and I know you finally feel fear. Surrender and we shall spare the children. Let me allow them to watch as I dispatch you and your servant spirits to purgatory, and then I will set them free. Surrender, outlaw, it is the only way." Kurt's voice was raspy and strained as the Goblin of Greed possessing him continued his rant, walking ahead of his army, taunting and laughing as he came. Robin reached for his bow but then looked once more at the face of the Polish boy, as innocent as his own protectors were, and realised that while he was determined to take as many evil souls with him as possible into limbo, the captured teens should be left unharmed so that they had some chance, at least, to escape.

Hua Mulan and Hongi Hika came closer to their leader's side as the army advanced. They, too, realised that this was the end and that the numbers before them were too great. Gouyen moved to the other side of the room in case the enemy decided to break in there. Despite the despair, Ada Lovelace was still smiling ruefully and told her friends to look at Leah who was kneeling in front of the door. Even with an injured arm, she was feverishly working, with Billy's help, to attach two wires to the door handle – two wires that led from the light switch. It was gratifying to watch the friends using their talents well, still with hope in their hearts. All the ghosts thought back in time, back to the feeling of being young, of being alive – how good those feelings had been.

And then Kurt stood a few feet from the door, still taunting and still laughing – the massed ranks of ghouls, criminals and boys ten feet behind him. "You disappoint me, Robin Hood. I thought you would come out to meet me like a man. Instead, you cower with your children. At least that arrogant whelp Arthur would have lost his temper and come to fight me on the battlefield."

The goblin leader, using Kurt's body, reached for the door handle just as Leah finished her task and stepped back. When the boy grabbed the knob to enter the house in triumph, the lights flashed once and Kurt was thrown backwards, his possessor tumbling down on the porch, cursing and shouting. But the flash in the house had not been the only sudden illumination and the members of the evil army were now looking towards the forest. There, an even brighter light had materialised. King Arthur had come riding out of the trees on a big, white stallion, with Mabel sitting up front clutching the grail. Behind them, twelve other men and horses galloped in line. Arthur charged his cavalry at the enemy horde; and as the horses scattered the ghouls, his knights leapt from the great beasts and flew inside the remaining Polish boys, dragging their possessors out with ease. They then left the exhausted young teens so they could attack the remaining ghouls with flashing blades and shouts of anger.

The enemy leader was now standing by the door, witnessing the destruction of his army. He did not see Gouyen come up behind him and did not see her plunge a knife deep into his back so that he erupted in flame and smoke and disappeared into oblivion; and he did not hear her words. "We are not servants of Robin Hood, fool. We are friends of Robin Hood."

The rout took a matter of minutes and, amazingly, the protectors were victorious. King Arthur came galloping up to the house and helped Mabel down. She immediately ran to hug Gouyen, the grail dangling in her hand. "Thank you for everything," she said.

"You are so welcome, my sister. And thank you for your bravery!" Gouyen replied.

King Arthur embraced his friend and fellow English legend and then he knelt in front of Gouyen, kissing her hand and bowing his head. Then all the protectors turned and entered the house together. Mabel walked forward to Emma and James who were still unconscious on the floor of the house. She was holding the silver cup with outstretched arms, eyes closed in deep prayer and then she got on her knees. She placed the grail on Emma's stomach, bringing up her listless arms and folding them around the prize so that she embraced it in her sleep. Immediately, the colour returned to her cheeks; she took a deep breath and her eyes opened. She looked up at her friend and then over at Robin Hood and King Arthur. And then she looked down at her arms.

"Is this what I think it is?" she asked. There was a mixture of tears and laughter in the room as Emma stood and repeated the process with James until they were both awake, laughing and crying.

Return to Sherwood Forest
One

Robin Hood was as focused and organised as ever, even after they had found the grail and either destroyed or run off all the enemy ghouls. Amid celebrations, and while Richard and Hippocrates were getting the help of the grail to first heal Leah and then the injured Polish boys on the battlefield, Robin declared that they had an hour to wrap up whatever tasks that were left before they had to leave. But there were not too many tasks. Medicine had never been easier for Hippocrates after Richard had found a freshwater spring near the edge of the forest and filled the grail to the brim. Then they just made everyone, patients and fighters alike, drink earth power infused liquid from the cup and wounds and fatigue could be seen disappearing before their very eyes. The process was equally effective on mental wounds. That became obvious after they had found Kurt lying curled up in a ball, not too far from the house with hands that were burned and a mind that was deeply scarred. Emma had cradled the boy's head in her lap as he had moaned, still amazed that they had stumbled upon a relative of her brother – which meant he was her cousin too. A forced sip from the cup and Kurt's moaning had stopped and then gradually his eyes had opened and a profound, if exhausted, look of peace had spread over his face.

James was walking and talking as though he had never been sick for a day in his life. This was due, of course, to the grail – the knowledge that he could now take the grail home to help his father and because he had been introduced to the Knights of the Round Table. He was living every teenage boy's dream but then all the protectors felt a little like they were in dreamland. They had achieved their goal – a goal that had once seemed so far-fetched – and everyone had played their part. It was truly a team effort. Whether it was planning, fighting, collaborating or healing – everyone had a good story to tell. And they did. Robin Hood was aware of the need to unwind and gave his young friends time to share their tales, which they did with gusto.

King Arthur had an integral description to provide – one that was needed to fill in gaps in the overall story – but he would not tell it. It was up to James to recall his memories of the final battle that had taken place in his body before he blacked out. He had an insider's view of the king's role as a saviour that no one else had seen. He recalled images of Arthur and the Goblins of Greed being sucked up and away from him, along a dark and frightening tunnel that led into the sky. One ghoul was screaming in agony and frustration: agony because he had Excalibur buried to the hilt in his stomach; frustration because he had not succeeded in stealing the grail and because he was now heading for purgatory where he knew he would spend many years in limbo. The second ghoul was struggling and choking because Arthur had him in a vicious headlock. The king was as focused on victory as ever but also wore a pained expression. He had defeated his enemies, but James had been greatly harmed. He had removed two great demons from the battlefield but was not on the battlefield to help his friends. He had managed to create a free path for Mabel to the grail but was on his way to limbo and so would not be able to see or experience victory if it happened.

"I am certainly not the hero. You are all heroes. Leah, where would we have been without your scientific knowledge? Billy, you fought like a demon on so many occasions. Richard, you are a born healer and there would have been oceans of pain without you. Emma and James, I cannot imagine where we would be without your leadership and the ordeal you survived, being possessed by monsters from Underworld. All heroes."

"Mabel, I do not leave you out. You, above all, taught me something. I think, perhaps, you have felt alone for some time. But the connection you made, the relationship you built with Gouyen so quickly, the fact she felt like sharing powerful magic with you when she barely knew you, that is what saved us. In purgatory, I was suddenly able to sense what was going on in our battle, send a message to my knights in the Otherworld telling them about our need, understand the urgency of confronting Mordred, see a pathway back to Earth – all because of the mystical connection you made with a wise woman of the Apache nation."

The Pachamama Protectors could have dwelt on King Arthur's words for days and could have continued telling stories for days more but Robin Hood was their leader and he insisted they prepare themselves to leave. "I, too, wish we could relax, enjoy, give appropriate thanks to those who deserve thanks, but our quest is not over and I think we will all not be completely safe – the grail will not be completely safe – until it sits at the heart of Loxley Chase. And, remember, the work of the grail is not done. We have a father to save also."

Those were words that spurred all into action despite physical and mental fatigue. Emma and James were the reason the quest existed in the first place; and all the protectors had met Mr Trueman and wanted him to be well again. It was time to move on. The group that left the forest and returned to the city of Brest was a different group – a team with additional questers. The friends and their companions still made up the core of the team, with Robin Hood as their leader, but King Arthur had convinced key members of his Knights of the Round Table to stay to help – to escort them back to England. Gawain, Lancelot and Perceval – all joined them on the journey while Sir Galahad, bravest and boldest of Arthur's friends, agreed to remain in the Białowieża Forest as its protector, along with Robin Hood's staff – an earth power vessel.

"We will not make the same mistake again. We cannot be complacent with our planet's future. Thank you, Galahad, for taking on this task." Robin Hood bowed to his friend as they left him.

The Pachamama Protectors continued to feel contentment and happiness after their victory, as they walked away together from the trees over the open scrubland. The quest was back on track, with ghosts hidden inside the protectors, Knights of the Round Table making themselves invisible and Robin Hood leading the way. It was like the moment they had first left Loxley

Chase with an epic journey ahead of them.

That sense of satisfaction was dampened, however, when they realised why Robin Hood had been so anxious to leave Białowieża quickly. As they entered the series of alleys and streets again, it felt like the danger present in Brest had grown, not lessened. Thieves and thugs were out in force – individuals and groups roaming the city. Some were just intent on causing mayhem, but others seemed to be looking for the Pachamama Protectors, following them as they tried to quickly make an escape. When the railway station came into view – with a burning, gutted wreckage of a locomotive on the tracks surrounded by a mob smashing windows and looting the carriages – it became clear that they still had work to do to get back home.

But they were now a seasoned fighting force. The children didn't feel like children; they felt like warriors – and they had legends and knights by their side. Angry mobs were one thing, but when a gang of thugs tried to attack the protectors and their friends, they were sent packing quickly with flaming arrows and swinging blades. Direct assailants were not the only obstacles slowing them down in their attempt to return to Loxley, though. The overall chaos that had erupted in Brest was more of an impediment. The city seemed to be falling into full riot mode with fires in buildings, glass shattered all around them and wrecked cars on the roads.

"I thought we would be safe with the grail, that our journey home would be easy?" James was bewildered as he followed Robin Hood down smoky streets and pathways.

King Arthur appeared, walking beside his companion

for a while. "We have taken the grail from a place where it has been hidden for hundreds of years, James. That act was never going to be peaceful. Galahad will help restore some order here, but I fear these scenes will soon be repeated in other regions around the world if we are not successful. The planet is unbalanced. Climate change is advancing, two earth power vessels are missing and dark magic is brewing in the Otherworld. We need to restore hope."

There were thoughtful looks on the faces of friends and ghosts alike as Arthur concluded; and they continued their journey. Perhaps the king inspired them because that was when Leah and Ada Lovelace came up with an idea to escape the chaos. The girl beckoned to her friends to follow and she led them to a large open lot, next to a shopping complex. It had all manner of vehicles for sale or rent. "I know I'm only fourteen, but my parents allow me to pull their car into the garage at night and Ada says she understands the combustion engine. Why don't we take one of these camper vans?"

When Leah pointed at a large Ford motorhome, Robin Hood nodded enthusiastically and they all ran towards it just as a gas main exploded behind them. James signalled to Lancelot to follow him into the showroom; and as they entered through the doors, the knight made himself visible and a salesclerk screamed and dived under his desk. James knelt and made it clear he was a real boy, not a ghost, and when the clerk calmed down, he explained quickly and clearly which set of keys he needed as Lancelot loomed over his shoulder. Quick as a flash, they were back with their friends in the motorhome and Leah was starting the engine.

Two

The big van hummed into life and an electricity pole came crashing down to the ground in front of them. As the young protector tried to remember how to reverse the vehicle out of the lot onto the road, she realised she had a big problem. The van was a stick shift and her legs were too short to reach the pedals. She spoke quickly to Ada Lovelace who seemed unfazed by the issue. In a flash, she had extended her own spiritual legs through Leah's feet and suddenly the gears were engaged, the accelerator was floored and they were rushing backwards out onto a main street. Equally as quickly, gears were changed again and the motorhome was squealing forward, leaving rubber and smoke on the tarmac. Before any of the group could pick themselves off the floor, they were flying between buildings and debris, heading for the outskirts of the city – hoping to find some semblance of order and freedom.

And, remarkably, they did break free of the chaos with impressive speed. There was time for the friends to sit back in their seats, for the ghosts to marvel at the vehicle they were in and for the Pachamama Protectors to take a moment to reflect that they were heading for Loxley. Emma and James hugged and James unashamedly began to cry again as he thought of his father back home in the hospital. Robin Hood had given him his word that Mr Trueman would be alive if they returned, and while he had absolute faith in their leader, still he worried. Ada Lovelace had found and toyed with a GPS system in the van, and she showed why she was a revered mathematician by making it work and mapping out a route across Europe that would take them home by road. There were some more signs of unrest around them as they saw several groups of looters and vandals, but the ghosts seemed to have a sixth sense for trouble ahead, especially Hippocrates, and he would direct Leah to make many turns and twists onto back roads and side streets which allowed them to skirt most of the major issues.

The children slept for a while on two pull-out beds at the back of the van, taking turns to lay down to sleep fully or sit in a chair to doze fitfully. They were all exhausted, physically and mentally drained from their ordeal, but it was a satisfied exhaustion – a feeling of fatigue that had been earned and had led to success. When they were somewhat recovered, they asked more questions of the ghosts and listened to stories from the new members of the group. The Knights of the Round Table were pleased to be back amongst the living and weaved together magical tales from the past that enlightened and entertained everyone. Then they all turned to more serious matters and Robin Hood painted a picture of the weeks and months that lay ahead if they were to continue with their efforts to save the world.

"We have a long drive ahead of us, so we will not celebrate too soon. But my heart tells me that we have been successful in our quest. The grail will soon sit in Yorkshire and the full rebirth of Sherwood Forest will begin. Białowieża has a new vessel and a new protector.

You are all to be congratulated, my friends, but I think you see and sense that our work is not done. Before this quest, before you, our protectors, were recruited, the enemy was close to victory. They had successfully captured two containers, full of nature's power and had a plan to steal the greatest vessel of all – the grail. If they achieved that, they could sit back and watch as mankind continued to fuel climate change and all the great forests of the world withered and died. They could capture the last of the stored power, take it to the astral plane and their battle to control the Underworld would truly begin while planet Earth became a barren wasteland."

"But victory is not clear to them any more. The grail is safe; it is in the hands of the good. Our evil foes have seen the strength of the Pachamama Protectors. They face the prospect of defeat – of health returning to Earth, of trees and plants growing instead of dying. Believe me, they will be enraged; and they will fight."

Hua Mulan leaned forward in her seat to add some words to Robin Hood's prophecy.

"You have done so well, my friends. We should be heartened; we should revel in this victory and then we should prepare. As Robin Hood has said, for the near future, we have secured Białowieża and will have secured Sherwood. We must make a plan to aid the kauri tree in New Zealand and the giant redwood in North America where earth power is still present, and to replant the baobab in Kenya and the banyan tree in the Amazon. Plus, we must risk great peril by entering the Darkworld – the nether reaches of the astral plane to reclaim the stolen artefacts. Ah, there are trying times ahead."

All the ghosts had left their companions and now stood or sat in full view of the children, bringing them calm and inspiration as Robin Hood and Hua Mulan brought them reality. Even Ada Lovelace had stood after finding a cruise control button which left Leah alone to steer a path back to England along the wide highways that covered Germany. The protectors looked at the legends and the legends looked at the protectors; and there was love and respect on both sides. The future that had been described was disturbing but hopeful nonetheless, more than hopeful, because of the individuals that sat in a camper van, speeding across Europe, heading for the short-term safety of their island home. Arthur beckoned to Mabel and she stood, brought forward the grail and then the king filled the cup with simple bottled water.

"Let us all drink from this sacred chalice, infused with green vitality – dead and living alike. Let us drink and let us swear another oath. We will not rest, will not lay down our arms unless we find ourselves lost and helpless in purgatory. We will not rest until our world is safe again, our Earth lives and breathes and the creatures and plants of this Earth live and breathe. We will not rest until our evil enemies in the Darkworld are thwarted. Let us take an oath to hard work and pain and fury in the name of peace. Let us take an oath to the Pachamama Protectors!"

And the grail was passed from mouth to mouth and all who sipped from the cup spoke the oath and felt peace and warmth flow through their bodies.

Three

The return of the protectors to real life and the replacement of the substitute spirits with actual boys and girls had been easier than they thought. They had worried about their parents finding out about the trick, seeing obvious differences while they were away or seeing double when they tried to switch back, being traumatised by the sight of their children standing next to their fake children. But Robin Hood had just taken them to Loxley Chase and put out a silent call and while it took a few hours for the spirits to sneak away without causing concern, eventually all the stand-ins came walking into the clearing to sit in front of their real-life doubles.

Robin asked for reports and stories were told of homework finished, football games won or lost and of parents being concerned about the flu virus that seemed to be spreading through the village. There were no indications of discovery. The report was brief and the spirits sucked back into the living quickly because Emma and James were anxious to leave, to go to the hospital with the grail hidden in a duffel bag.

"All will be well, my friends; all will be well." Hua Mulan smiled as they prepared to go, to run as fast as possible to the hospital. The brother and sister paused and looked once more at the assembled ghosts who all wished them luck. They were great men and women – great men and women who had achieved much throughout history – but were humble enough to understand the concern felt for a sick loved one. Emma and James thought one more time how lucky they had been when they stumbled into Loxley Chase – the haunted wood. Look at the friends they had made! Robin Hood, King Arthur, Hua Mulan, Gouyen, Ada Lovelace and Hippocrates. And now the Knights of the Round Table. Truly remarkable.

They ran nonstop through the trees, down the hill, through streets and doorways and hallways until they reached their father's room. Emma pushed open the door and stopped, taking a long deep breath to calm herself. There, on the bed, lay the husk of a man, skinny, barely breathing, heart barely beating with a nurse next to him adjusting an IV; and sitting next to the bed was their mother, crying and sobbing.

Their mother looked up. "I thought I told you both to stay at home. You had your last visit with him. You cannot watch this. Please go!" She was hysterical and James went to her and wrapped his arms around her, comforted her while Emma went around to the other side of the bed and moved the startled nurse aside with surprising ease. The girl reached down and took out what seemed like a simple silver cup from her bag and laid it on her father's chest. There were a few moments of silence as everyone in the room looked expectantly at the sick man. Their mother and the nurse—neither had any idea what the chalice was, or why the children had brought it.

But, still, they paused because they could sense something powerful in the air, something that might help a man who was essentially already dead. James was squeezing his mother's hand, lips moving rapidly as he said Robin Hood's name, followed by the words 'you promised', over and over. Only Emma was relaxed now – now that she had reached her father and had given him the grail. She had a big smile on her face and the smile grew wider still when her father opened his eyes and looked from side to side. As he saw his family around him, a tear appeared and trickled down his cheek and his chest rose and fell, releasing a breath that was also a sigh of relief.

A Storm is Coming
One

Mr Trueman recovered with remarkable speed. To the doctors and nurses in the cancer hospital, it was a miracle. To Mr and Mrs Trueman, it was a miracle. Within weeks, both parents had stopped into the school to talk with the headmaster to discuss when they could begin teaching again. The return to normality in some ways seemed wrong to the adults. To go from despair and death's door to extreme happiness seemed like too much of a dream. Interestingly, while they recognised their own wounds – the physical and mental scars, the practical consequences of the illness in bills and repairs needed to the house, relationships that had to be rebuilt with friends and relatives – Mr and Mrs Trueman could not see any scars present on their own children. On the contrary, they both seemed to have grown, physically but also in strength of character and depth of wisdom. This manifested itself in the way the parents were spoken to, supported and comforted. It felt like they had friends of equal age in the house when they returned home, rather than a son and daughter.

One Saturday morning, Emma and James asked their father if he would like to walk with them through the village. Mr Trueman had an exercise routine now, as he tried to regain his strength and endurance, but usually he went for gentle strolls away from Loxley after the children had left for school or while they were doing homework. The thought of walking with them into the village itself was appealing and so they set off, laughing, talking and waving at neighbours who were out working in their gardens – washing their cars or walking their dogs on what was a warm, late winter day. Mr Trueman commented on how alive the village looked. He had always been proud of Loxley and its uniqueness, but this was something extra special. It was still early in the new year, but flower beds seemed to be blooming, bushes stretching wide and tall, green leaves unfurling early on trees. There was a smell of vitality in the air and Mr Trueman could not figure out if there was something strange occurring or if his newfound health had allowed him to sense this vitality anew. He was a nature lover but could not remember loving nature more.

Love of the natural world was one thing, but when they reached the bottom of Loxley Hill on their walk and his children suggested they carry on up to the wood, Mr Trueman hesitated. He was not a superstitious man or an irrational man; still, he had heard the tales of Loxley Chase. He had never been close to the trees; he had hardly ever looked at the trees. He just knew they were intimidating. But for whatever reason, his children pleaded and begged – and after all, he had just recovered from cancer, just climbed out of a deathbed – so he took a deep breath and walked. The incline was surprisingly steep and it took his breath away initially and then he felt a second wind and also felt again that scent of green life in the air. A spring returned to his step and before he knew it, he was at the top of the hill.

Mr Trueman took a deep breath. The trees looked and felt like all the other plants in the village – fresh, full of new leaves and growing branches. Even on the grassland outside the boundary of the wood, there were seedlings sprouting as though Loxley Chase itself was expanding outwards. The three family members stood for a while, looking out at the village below. Emma and James stared with familiarity while their father observed with newfound appreciation. He had never been to this spot before, but the view was breathtaking. He had always known they lived in a beautiful part of the country, but this confirmed it. He could have stayed on the hill for hours but there were black clouds on the horizon – on the distant horizon way out to the west. It looked like a storm was coming. Also, while he felt uplifted by the experience of standing next to Loxley Chase with his children, he still felt just a little apprehensive. It was as though something was watching him, looking out from the trees behind him. He didn't say anything but just asked his children if they could leave and so, down the hill they went, winding back through the village, back to their house where Mr Trueman could rest and perhaps take a nap.

When Emma and James had safely escorted their father back home, they sprinted out of the house, raced through the streets – waving at bewildered individuals who had seen them moments before – and galloped up Loxley Hill, straight into the trees. There, just out of sight stood their friends with big smiles on their faces.

"Your father looks like a good man." Hua Mulan and Ada Lovelace both hugged the children.

"And he looks very well – very strong considering…"

Hippocrates was so happy for his young friends. He was pleased whenever he observed improvement in a patient.

Robin Hood, King Arthur and Hongi Hika were also happy but anxious too. The archer had been the one who had asked if Emma and James could bring their father to the edge of the wood so that the ghosts could see him. The young protectors spoke about his recovery often, but it was not the same as seeing it, not the same as seeing the man himself – the person who had been an intricate part of the quest, one reason they had embarked on the quest. But while the warriors in the group were pleased to see the children, they also had a grimness in their eyes, eyes that flicked constantly towards the horizon. Emma noticed the glances and looked out over the village at the distant sky. It really was a gorgeous day. Blue stretched almost as far as the eye could see and then disappeared into blackness.

"It's coming, isn't it? The storm is coming." Emma reached out and took her brother's hand as she spoke.

"It is coming, too quickly, too soon. If only those were rain clouds. We will need to leave soon." Robin was frowning but then shook his head and smiled again. "But, look to the north, see how the grail works its magic already."

Emma and James stepped out of the trees and looked north, towards the cities of Barnsley and, further away, Leeds. Up until recently, a series of factories had led right up to the border of their village. They had stretched back into an industrial complex and then rows of houses that became Barnsley. Now, however, there were big cranes and backhoes close to them – on the edge of Loxley itself.

"What is that? What's happening?" James was

surprised they hadn't heard anything about a new building project.

Ada Lovelace put her hand on the boy's shoulder. "A landowner from Sheffield decided to buy up those old factories so he could develop a county park. Apparently, he just suddenly started thinking about how few green spaces there were left that his grandchildren could visit, so he decided to level those buildings to connect parkland with Loxley Chase. He came up to visit us last week and we just kept out of his way. I heard him say he had been warned about visiting the wood but didn't understand what the fuss was about."

All the ghosts laughed and then King Arthur beckoned them back into the trees. As he did so, Emma noticed for the first time a new ghost – a young ghost standing back in the shade, next to a big, thick old oak. He was a boy, perhaps her age, with long blond hair pulled into a knot behind his head. Then, on the other side of the tree, she saw another boy – a living one this time. It was Kurt. The king saw her looking and waved to the brother and sister again.

"Sorry, Emma and James, I forgot to introduce a friend. This is Derfel. He wanted to come and see if he could help in some way – perhaps prepare you for your upcoming journey. He is obviously very familiar with the Otherworld. And, of course, you know Kurt." Both children smiled at the boys, and they smiled back. Emma wondered at Derfel's age, wanted to hear his story, why he had ended up in heaven when he was so young. And James, of course, wanted to spend time with a cousin he had never met. But before either of them could ask questions, King Arthur led them all away, deeper into the wood.

They followed the now familiar trail and marvelled again at all the new buds and shoots in the bushes and grasses, along with rabbits, foxes, squirrels and birds. There was an undoubted vibrancy in the air and the reason, of course, was revealed as they entered the enclosure. Emma was reminded of the clearing in Białowieża Forest – now more than ever – because in the middle of their Loxley Chase gathering place, the logs had been placed in a circle and in the centre, on a simple wooden stand, stood the grail. It didn't shine or hum, or vibrate in any way, just stood. But it was beautiful; and the friends – children and ghosts alike – sat for a while, just to stare.

Printed in the USA
CPSIA information can be obtained
at www.ICGtesting.com
LVHW040759080424
776736LV00003B/113